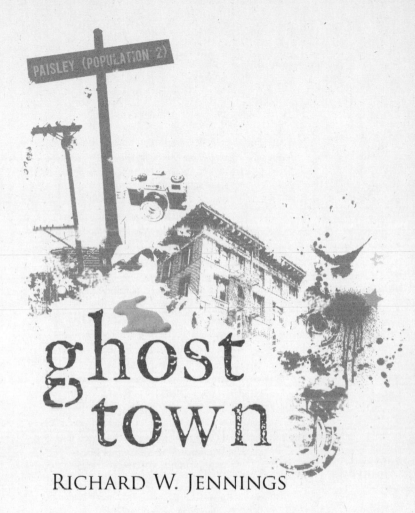

ghost
town

RICHARD W. JENNINGS

Houghton Mifflin

Houghton Mifflin Harcourt

Boston • New York • 2009

Houghton Mifflin is an imprint of
Houghton Mifflin Harcourt Publishing Company.

www.hmhbooks.com

The text of this book is set in Garamond.

Library of Congress Cataloging-in-Publication Data
Jennings, Richard W. (Richard Walker), 1945–
Ghost town / Richard W. Jennings.
p. cm.
Summary: Thirteen-year-old Spencer Honesty and his
imaginary friend, an Indian called Chief Leopard Frog, improbably
achieve fame and riches in the abandoned town of Paisley, Kansas,
when Spencer begins taking photographs with his deceased father's
ancient camera and Chief Leopard Frog has his poems published
by a shady businessman in the Cayman Islands.
ISBN 978-0-547-19471-4
[1. Ghost towns—Fiction. 2. Business enterprises—Fiction.
3. Imaginary playmates—Fiction. 4. Kansas—Fiction.
5. Humorous stories.] I. Title.
PZ7.J4298765Gh 2009
[Fic]—dc22
2008036781

Printed in the United States of America
MP 10 9 8 7 6 5 4 3 2 1

TO MY BROTHERS

William Karl Jennings III
Robert Nelson Jennings

Acknowledgments

THE AUTHOR EXTENDS his gratitude to Walter Lorraine, formerly vice president and publisher, Walter Lorraine Books, Houghton Mifflin Company, Boston, for his early encouragement of this work; to Stacy Graham O'Connell, formerly editor, Walter Lorraine Books, Houghton Mifflin Company, for her insights and friendship; to Erica Zappy, associate editor, Houghton Mifflin Harcourt Children's Books, for her skillful and unflappable stewardship of this project; to Susan Cohen, agent, the Writer's House, New York, for her accomplished management of the many details that remain beyond this author's capabilities; to Hannah Meyer and Brandi Polson for volunteering to help edit the original manuscript; to Tim Engle, acting editor, *Star Magazine*, the *Kansas City Star,* for daring to serialize this story each week for forty-two weeks during 2008–9; to Daniel C. Fitzgerald, author of *Ghost Towns of Kansas: A Traveler's Guide* and *Faded Dreams: More Ghost Towns of Kansas* (University Press of Kansas) for helping to inform this fictional account of the last kid in a dying Kansas town. My thanks to you all.

Richard W. Jennings
Overland Park, Kansas

"What's the rush?"

The Last Goodbye

"WELL, I GUESS THAT MAKES IT OFFICIAL," I said to Chief Leopard Frog.

Oil-stained gravel crunched beneath the eighteen big tires of the Mayflower moving van. A volley of green walnuts clattered into the ditch as the heavily laden transport made a wide right turn onto Highway 99, followed by the entire Balderson family in their faded silver Yukon.

"I am now the last kid in Paisley, Kansas."

Already, a spider had begun to form a web on the Balderson mailbox, the first of three mismatched rusting galvanized steel boxes that stood in a crooked row atop hand-cut post rocks like sentries dozing on duty.

Somehow, animals know.

This one, a big, fat yellow and black garden spider, dangled in the late-summer calm before tossing a sticky lasso to the tombstone-shaped door that for years had creaked open to bring Tim Balderson his monthly video game magazine.

It is well known that our lives hang by such a thread.

It is less understood that the lives of entire towns do.

First the factory closes, its working parts stripped and shipped overseas.

Then the able-bodied people who own no land decide to try their luck someplace else.

Foreclosed-on mobile homes are trucked away like coyotes skulking through the night.

The few children who live in regular houses are bussed thirty miles away to school, and one by one, the shops, the café, the gas station, and the old folks disappear as if there'd been a great abduction by creatures from outer space.

The last to vanish are the grain elevator and the post office.

Since my mother is the letter carrier contractor, the very last wagon out of town most likely will include me.

In all the time I've lived in Paisley, Kansas, which is since the blessed moment thirteen years and five days ago when I was born, only one person has ever returned, and he's not real.

Chief Leopard Frog was my imaginary friend when I was three or four or five years old. I don't remember exactly. Details from early childhood don't lend themselves to being summoned on demand from the caves of memory.

Chief Leopard Frog taught me to identify native wildflowers and to sense pending changes in the weather by listening to the southwest wind. He showed me how to build a hideout using only sod, sticks, and chunks of limestone.

It was Chief Leopard Frog who helped me through those cold empty patches of time after my grandfather died, and Chief Leopard Frog who told me all those stories of unseen spirits when I lay in bed so long, suffering from the fever.

One day, shortly after I started going to school, Chief Leopard Frog moved on, presumably to lend a hand to some other kid.

But last year, not long after the hailstorm that got the crops, and the EVERYTHING MUST GO sale at the Country Mart Food and

Drug, and the sudden, whispered-about passing of Mr. Walker at the bank, Chief Leopard Frog came back.

I found him sitting on my porch when the school bus dropped me off. He was whittling a talisman from a burl he'd found. He said he knew it would bring me luck because the burl had come from an active bee tree.

I was glad to have it, because to tell the truth, I wasn't feeling very lucky at the time.

Tim Balderson was not my best friend. Frankly, I liked his sister, Maureen, better. But Tim was my age and Maureen was two years older. Also, they were the only other kids left. Without them, I had only my books.

Several years ago there was a bookstore in Paisley—Louise Franks & Company, Bookseller—but Mrs. Franks's shop was an early victim of the Paisley curse. When she closed for good, which was about the same time that the shoe store and the barbershop left, and Mrs. Franks moved to Emporia to live with her sister, she gave me a big carton of paperback books from which the covers had been torn off. It was like receiving canned food without labels. Every time I opened one, it was a surprise.

My favorite from Mrs. Franks's parting largesse was a novel about three dogs that joined forces to write rhyming poetry. Eventually, they collectively became the poet laureate of the United States, although no one ever knew that there were three dogs involved. Everybody thought there was just one. I thought the book was funny. Also, it made me wish I had a dog, but my mother said that taking on the responsibility for another life at this time would be "the height of folly."

Chief Leopard Frog agreed with my mother, although the words he used were "Only the starving owl hunts in the thunderstorm."

I read every book that Mrs. Franks left behind.

This made me wish that Paisley had a library.

When I grow up and am rich, I will start a library in Paisley, if Paisley ever comes back.

Or if I ever do.

My Lucky Charm

The last kid left in Paisley, Kansas.

Man, oh, man.

How can I explain a life in which one's closest friends have tails? Or exoskeletons? Or compound eyes?

This was my life after the Baldersons moved to Kansas City. Insects, arachnids, grass-loving reptiles, ground-dwelling mammals—these became my acquaintances after the people departed. Not that I ever depended all that much on the indigenous people, other than my mother, but it was reassuring to be around someone with whom I had a common language.

Before Mr. Walker died so suddenly, he and I would talk about baseball in Kansas City. Before Mrs. Franks moved on, we would discuss the lives of writers such as Hemingway, Wolfe, Fitzgerald, Steinbeck, Proust, and Sinclair Lewis.

My mother read, but what she read were addresses and postmarks and contradictory directives from the United States Postal Service. When she'd get home from her rounds in the late afternoon, all she wanted to do was watch TV. Game shows. People arguing. *Oprah.*

I never knew my father. He died working in the fields a month before I was born. I wear his hat. It's a ball cap with an embroidered logo that says CATFISH, honoring a minor-league baseball team from my father's hometown of Columbus, Georgia.

It has his sweat stains.

It fits me perfectly.

Except for a few classroom assignments having to do with famous people from history (James Whitcomb Riley, for example, and William Allen White), I've never written anything except what you hold in your hands. I mention this because I'm hoping that whoever reads this journal will be sympathetic to the fact that I had to figure out a lot of things as I went along.

For instance, at what point should I tell you my name? For the record, it's Spencer Adams Honesty. My friends—ha, ha!—call me Spence. I say "ha, ha!" because there's nobody left in Paisley to call me anything at all, except my mother, who doesn't need to use a name since I'm the only other person in the room.

"Here," she'll say, "take this out to the trash barrel and burn it."

There's certainly no need for her to add "Spence, dear" to her instruction. Who else could she possibly be talking to?

Under these circumstances, it's easy to forget that I have a name.

If I'd ever gotten a dog, I suppose I'd have called him "Here, boy," because what's the point of identifying differences using names if there's nothing left to differentiate?

Sometimes I'd sit on the front porch and name the hummingbirds. Ruby. Flicker. Buzzy. Emerald. But this was a meaningless exercise since I was the only one who knew who each one was and they were incapable of understanding the names I'd given them.

When I'd say, "Come here, Ruby," they all would show up, or not, as the case may be.

So things in Paisley, Kansas, simply became things.

Names no longer mattered.

The talisman that Chief Leopard Frog carved for me was in the shape of a rabbit. From nose to tail, it was two and one quarter inches long, and from feet to tips of ears, it was one and one half inches high. It was very smooth and the perfect size for a hand or pocket.

In some cultures, Chief Leopard Frog told me, such charms are called *netsukes*. They are sometimes carried in a pocket, as I prefer, and sometimes drilled so they can be worn on leather lanyards or golden necklaces.

They are almost always in the shape of protective animals, although tiny Buddhas are not uncommon.

It all depends on who's doing the carving and how he's feeling that day.

My talisman had big eyes, a prominent nose, and laid-back ears. His forelegs and haunches were merely suggested by the carver, but his tail was as carefully defined as a button for a shirt collar.

In the spirit of the gift, I carried that rabbit everywhere. My constant fidgeting and fiddling with him oiled his surface so each day he became a little darker, a little smoother.

How things work out depends a lot on luck.

And I had a real honest-to-goodness, handmade Native American lucky charm.

Or so—in my eagerness to see the bright side—I thought.

Pictures in My Mind

THEY CALL THEM ghost towns.

Those towns in Kansas and other parts of the Great Plains that once had as many as twenty thousand residents but today are nothing more than cornfields with a few inconvenient stones.

These are towns that were beat up by flooding streams, capricious tornadoes, hard-nosed managers at the railroads, unscrupulous lenders, and politicians in Topeka drawing lines on maps that placed the new highways too far away. Fires, drought, locusts, greed—all have taken their toll on what for some people was their whole world.

Entire towns that disappeared simply because of bad luck.

Ghost towns.

I rubbed my rabbit talisman. It felt solid, immutable, secure.

Should I tell you what I look like?

Does it matter?

I am five feet, three inches tall. I hope this isn't it as far as it goes for me. I would like to be taller.

Time will tell.

I have brownish-blond hair. It is very fine and wispy and hard to keep in place.

I have a brown mole on my right cheek. I hate it, but it's there, looking like a fat fly has just landed on me. When I am older, and rich, and have finished building a library for Paisley, I will have it surgically removed.

My teeth are straight, my eyes are brown, and my fingers are sort of stubby. If I had wanted to become a concert pianist, no matter how hard I might practice, I would never be able to reach all the chords, especially the ones demanded by Beethoven. He had really big hands, I understand, as did both James Whitcomb Riley and William Allen White.

I can run fast. I can lift bales of hay. Using an old, rusty five-iron that my father left behind in the barn, I once hit a golf ball into the lake from my front porch. I don't know how far that is, but at the time it seemed to qualify for a world record.

Maureen Balderson kissed me.

This was before she left, of course. I think she kissed me because there was nobody else to kiss, except her brother, and why would she want to do that? She also took her top off, which astonished me, but I didn't try to stop her. The summer sun illuminated her tiny breasts in the most shameless way. It made the kissing a lot more interesting.

I think Maureen is basically a nice person. But I think, too, that because she is two years older than I am, she has become somewhat confused about what she's supposed to be doing with her life.

Her brother, Tim, acted as if his sister didn't even exist. It was like even in tiny Paisley they lived in two completely different parts of town.

Maureen was a cute girl. She had freckles that I liked. They weren't just on her face, either, as I found out that day to my delight. They were all over. A girl covered from stem to stern with polka dots.

How lucky for her, I thought.

Now that she's gone, I think about her more than I probably should.

It gets hot in Kansas in the summertime.

The rain can wait months to return.

Fields wither. Insects buzz. Creeks shrink down to shards of pottery.

If you were foolish enough to sit down in the tall grass you would get up with ticks on your legs—or worse. That night, you would use tweezers and rubbing alcohol to carefully pull them out of your skin.

Ticks are nasty little animals, yet they seem to be doing better in Paisley than the rest of us.

Tim Balderson liked to hunt for frogs. After he'd find one, he would kill it, usually by throwing it like a baseball against a rock or a tree.

Horrified, I'd ask him, "Why do you do that?"

"I don't know," he'd answer. "It's just the hunter in me, I suppose."

There is no hunter in me. I figure life is too precarious to add my influence to who is going to be lucky and who isn't.

Chief Leopard Frog agrees.

He'd agree even if his last name weren't Frog.

"Let it be," he once told me in no uncertain words. "We're all equal in this world."

Maureen Balderson's nipples were tiny and pink. I wish now that I had taken a picture of her.

In fact, I wish I had a picture of everybody who has lived in Paisley, Kansas, since the day I was deposited here by the stork. At one time or another, they were all my friends.

But it's too late now.

Now, it's all in my mind.

Busy Hands Are Happy Hands

HERE'S AN INTERESTING FACT that says a lot about the way our government operates: Even though there was no one left in Paisley but my mother and me, and thus no one to deliver mail to but ourselves, my mother continued to be paid the same as always.

So she didn't feel awkward about receiving the money, she busied herself in the morning pasting forwarding stickers on the few letters that still arrived. Other mail, such as advertising circulars and catalogs, she put into a bin for paper recycling. Some of the envelopes and packages she stamped RETURN TO SENDER. But even when she took her time and tidied up after herself she was always finished before noon.

We had a lot of time on our hands, but although we are closely related and have deep affection for each other, I'm sure, our interests have always been dissimilar. For example, she likes to watch TV.

I can't sit still that long.

Long before the Baldersons moved to Kansas City, getting supplies had become a problem in Paisley. The nearest supermarket was an hour's drive. The nearest town with lots of stores and a movie theater and a hospital was more than two hours distant. So trips for food and household necessities generally happened only once a week, and we were careful to prepare a detailed list.

Chief Leopard Frog suggested that I begin a project, something that I could do with my hands.

"Like what?" I asked.

I'd already built a hideout, and there's very little that one boy can do to rescue a big, rocky, weedy farm.

"Consult your talisman," he instructed.

I reached into my pocket. The smooth, hard rabbit fit into the concave of my palm as if tailor-made for its folds and creases.

When I made a fist, the talisman disappeared inside, yet it filled all the available space.

This is an ingenious bit of woodcarving, I started to tell Chief Leopard Frog.

But when I looked up to speak to him, he was gone.

Initially, Chief Leopard Frog appeared to be right about the power of the talisman. It directed me between that period when I was deep in sleep and that sudden moment when I was fully awake, not with spoken words, but using silent communication, broadcasting only during the divide between life's two unequal worlds, transmitting extrasensory messages from the fragile, shrouded land of drifting images and distant music, that nocturnal interlude called middle dreams.

Take my picture, the talisman suggested.

After breakfast, I went out to the workshop to search through my father's things. It didn't take me long to find it. It was right there next to his rusty tackle box, a big, box-shaped bag of tan imitation leather, and both containers covered with a layer of gritty dust and dead roly-polys.

Inside were lots of loose parts, extra lenses, a couple of rolls of unspent film, a compact, collapsable tripod, circular metal pieces with a purpose I couldn't discern—some sort of hood, perhaps?

But there it was, floating in the middle of all these accessories, my father's old thirty-five-millimeter single-lens reflex camera.

When I picked it up, it felt like a serious tool, not like the lightweight miniature digital cameras people use these days.

This one had actual moving parts assembled by hand, and its lens, while maybe not as fine a lens as money could buy, was certainly as fine as my father could buy at the time.

It was also a versatile lens. At the flip of a thumb switch, it would convert from a focus of short telephoto range to macro mode. In other words, unlike with most snapshot cameras, with this one I could make photographs both at a distance and in extreme close-up.

Small things, like talismans and spiders and red clover flowers, were within my realm.

Naturally, the battery was dead and the film in the bag had long since expired. And doubtlessly, the camera needed a cleaning.

But it was a start.

As Chief Leopard Frog might have said but, to his credit, didn't, *A collection of a thousand bug pictures starts with a single caterpillar.*

Our next trip to town was two days away. I used this time to prepare the camera and to read the soiled manual that came with it. Frankly, I found many of the operating instructions confusing. While the camera imitates the physical structure of the human eye, it sees things differently.

Learning these differences and how to manipulate them can become a lifelong obsession.

Like painting, sculpture, dancing, writing, and music, if it takes constant practice and the exclusion of all else to get things right, then it qualifies as art.

And as the life of every great artist proves, once you've finally got it right, you've long since gone crazy.

Fire the First Shot

Going crazy.

Is it something that happens to artists because they are obsessed with a subject that's not "real"? Or is it because while they're pursuing their art, they're alone?

I thought about this while walking through the fields of August, occasionally stopping to pull a bur from my ankle or duck an aggressive grasshopper.

When you do stop to think about it, everybody lives alone, even the people who are jammed together in cities. I think that's why my mother watches TV all afternoon and into the night.

She doesn't want to admit that she's alone.

I found myself becoming somewhat excited about the project that lay ahead. The talisman, or the spirit behind the hand that carved it, had suggested that I begin to notice small things.

This was ironic, I thought, because here I was in a vast, empty place that stretched in every direction like the Milky Way, with rarely a living soul in sight.

One small boy in an entire abandoned town.

One small planet in a solar system.

But not Pluto, of course. They fired Pluto.

What jerks!

(To their credit, though, the astronomers who made the final, fateful decision to downgrade Pluto's former status as the outermost planet in our solar system to that of a wandering dirty iceberg at least had the decency to wait until the Kansan who discovered it had died.)

As I frequently say, our lives hang by a thread, even after death, apparently, and so, too, do the lives of entire towns.

This recurring thought brought to mind one of the more outstanding failures in Kansas, a ghost town called Silkville. It is a true story that I read in one of the books left to me by Mrs. Franks.

Located in Franklin County, Silkville was the brainchild of an unpopular but very rich Frenchman who in 1870 acquired three thousand acres on which he built mansions and factories and planted orchards and grapes and mulberry trees—silkworm food—and to which he persuaded forty families to cross the Atlantic to join him in a vast silk-producing enterprise. For a time his silk business was a major factor in the world market. But bad luck, the bane of all existence, eventually reduced the Frenchman's grand scheme to rubble. Today, all but a few ailanthus trees are gone.

What remains is less than a memory.

> *My name is Ozymandias, king of kings:*
> *Look on my works, ye mighty, and despair!*
> —Percy B. Shelley

> *Easy come, easy go.*
> —Chief Leopard Frog

> *Hey, don't look at me. I didn't do it.*
> —Spencer Honesty

Today, the world's greatest empire is Wal-Mart, and it was to one of the thousands of emporiums of that grand enterprise that I traveled with my mother to obtain camera batteries and film.

"We're running out of Windex anyway," she said. "And I'm sure I can always find a few other things we need."

No kidding! I thought as I looked around the place, stuffed to the gills with more than forty thousand items.

Every kid in China must be working day and night to keep Wal-Mart filled with "a few other things we need," a few of which, it turns out, we don't really need at all, like the fish-shaped key chain I bought.

When you push a button on its right fin, it tells redneck jokes. This extraordinary item on the clearance shelf was only two dollars, and I saved at least that much on the film, specially packaged in a BUY FOUR, GET THE FIFTH ROLL FREE wrapper. The batteries, on the other hand, seemed pretty expensive by comparison.

I suspect that Wal-Mart knows this.

Anyway, it was good to get away from the house for a while, and my mother seemed pleased with her purchases. On the long drive home we talked about some of the families who'd moved away.

"I think the last straw was when they closed the school," my mother observed. "They might as well have ordered every family out of town right then and there. Of course, the handwriting was on the wall the day they closed the factory."

"What did they make at the factory?" I asked.

I was too young to recall Paisley's heyday.

"Plastic novelties," she answered. "You know, what some people call five-and-dime items. Imitation flowers, loaded dice, talking key chains, an eight-ball that tells your fortune when you turn it upside down—things like that. At one time, Paisley Plastics was the biggest plastic novelty manufacturer in the world."

"Things change," I observed.

"Mmm-hmm," my mother responded, switching on the radio, an indication that our conversation was over.

After a couple of false starts, I managed to make a photographic exposure of my talisman. The eyepiece of the camera shows exactly what the lens sees, so while I composed my shot, I was captivated by the object's detail. It was sort of like looking at pond water through a microscope. I saw things that I would never notice otherwise.

This was one fine piece of work.

Quite an achievement for an imaginary friend.

A Mix-Up in the Mail?

THROUGH THE MACRO LENS of my late father's camera, the rabbit talisman was a wonder to behold.

Chief Leopard Frog had carved my name in tiny letters underneath the rabbit's right paw (albeit with a minor typo, "Spender" instead of "Spencer"), and its nose, previously the rounded tip of the burl, was polished smoother than a cat's-eye marble.

Tiny whiskers no bigger than a human eyelash were suggested by a few carefully placed, nearly invisible scrapes.

Honestly, the more I examined my talisman, the more impressed I was with Chief Leopard Frog's talent.

With the ability to see into a fairy world, I had no need to travel far to exhaust a twenty-four-exposure roll of film.

I shot the star-shaped flowers in the pumpkin patch close enough to get their bright yellow powdery pollen on my face.

I took a picture of the marigold growing by itself near the front step. Its tiny overlapping petals filled the frame from edge to edge.

Just for the heck of it, I photographed a gum wrapper that had lain undisturbed on the ground for months, its letters faded, like Paisley itself, but still legible. I planned to title that one "Gum, but Not Forgotten."

Caterpillars had decimated the tomato crop. From a normal perspective, they looked like ugly lime green slugs, but when I saw the first one through the macro lens, I discovered that it had a stumpy red tail, curved like a hornet's stinger, ten suckerlike feet, such as an octopus has, plus half a dozen extra little sucker hands positioned just behind its big cabbage-colored head, pale oval eyes that seemed painted on like cartoon eyes, and sixteen bigger, darker fake eyes along both sides of its body.

If such a creature had stepped from a spacecraft and said, "People of Earth, we come in peace," I could not have been more astonished.

I shot several pictures from many angles.

Soon I began to enjoy the reassuring *click-thunk* sound that the big camera made each time I took a shot. Through my fingertips, I could feel the lens open and shut. Because it invisibly captured whatever it was aimed at, the camera reminded me of the mechanical ghost-catching device in the movie *Ghostbusters*. Only later, after it was properly emptied, would I find out what was inside.

Little did I know how prescient was my fleeting choice of metaphor.

My new hobby required patience.

Since Paisley had all but disappeared and Wal-Mart was an hour away—a destination limited to weekly trips—I figured the best way to get my pictures processed was through the mail.

From the recycling bin in my mother's office I chose among dozens of mail-order film-developing companies that routinely solicited business from people who had died or moved away from Paisley. The closest service used a post office box in St. Louis, so it was to the Sparkle Snapshot Company that I sent my first roll of film.

A lot of things change when you live alone.

Time, of course, is among the biggest. Days go by in which nothing worth mentioning happens. It's not that they're all the same. I imagine that if I were floating on a raft across the Pacific Ocean my ship's log might read a lot like my life in Paisley:

Hot today. Caught a fish.

Cloudy but still hot. Saw a seagull.

Another hot day. A truck went down the road, turned around, and went back the way it had come. Must be lost.

Another hot day. No rain expected. After bedtime, heard coyotes howling.

Watched a hawk catch a skink. Not easy.

And so on.

With no other people around, it's easy to let your appearance suffer. Certainly there's no need to dress up. Daily bathing becomes optional, too. You could give yourself a haircut if you wanted to, but what's the rush?

Thus, by degrees, people slip into a barbarous state.

"All the more reason to practice your art," Chief Leopard Frog urged. "Art lifts you up and separates you from the lower species."

The return of my first roll of film after ten days of waiting stimulated a Christmas-like feeling. My hands shook as I held the fat yellow envelope.

What if my pictures were no good?

But I needn't have worried. Except for the first two exposures, which were simply red streaks against a dark gray background, each of the images that followed was crisp, clear, and colorful. Yellow flowers. Green multieyed, multilegged monsters. A sprig of hay that looked like a cactus in the desert. The talisman's shiny nose and laid-back ears. A faded gum wrapper.

But then, the last picture in the stack startled me so much that I actually jumped up from my chair.

It was a snapshot of Tim Balderson's sister, Maureen, combing her hair!

What in the world? I thought.

Somehow, Sparkle Snapshot in St. Louis had managed to mix in a picture meant for the Baldersons.

Oh, well, I thought. *Nobody's perfect.*

The Third Mailbox

FOLLOWING A LONG DRY SPELL, a thunderstorm finally passed through Paisley, too late to save the corn crop, but with nearly four inches of welcome precipitation in twenty-four hours, the creeks overflowed and the pastures turned from brown to green overnight. The pumpkin patch, previously a tangle of knotted, brittle vines, suddenly sprang out in every direction like kudzu.

Chipmunks, possums, raccoons, and foxes came out from hiding to get a long, cold drink; birds lined up on the telephone wire to dry their wings; spiders repaired webs; and a turtle poked his head up from the pond to see what all the commotion was about.

I figured this might be a good time to take another set of pictures. I had to ration my film because film and developing are expensive—one roll is a full week's allowance—but after a hard rain the color of the landscape changes, the miniature population explodes, and things bloom as if they've been waiting for this moment all season.

I put on my dad's Columbus Catfish cap, slung my camera over my shoulder, and headed up toward Ma Puttering's place. Hers is the third mailbox I mentioned before. Three in a row at the end of our driveway: the Baldersons', ours, and Ma Puttering's, whose forty acres starts where the gravel county road turns into a private dirt road with a FOR SALE sign wired to a creaky wooden gate. That sign has been there for at least three years, ever since Ma Puttering quietly passed away.

I remember her as a nice lady with a gray streak in her hair who kept a pack of dogs and once in a while made homemade blackberry jam just for me.

Her place has gone to ruin since then, however. Nowadays, it's home to an extended family of quarrelsome raccoons. Nobody's ever going to buy it. Nobody's ever going to buy anybody's house in Paisley.

What would be the point?

From a distance, Ma Puttering's house looks like a quaint, picturesque ivy-covered cottage, but when you get a little closer you can see that the corner of the roof by the chimney has collapsed, a number of windows are cracked or broken out entirely, and the ivy isn't ivy at all but a huge mass of pumpkin vines that just keep on reseeding themselves year after year.

I switched my camera from macro mode to regular and took a portrait of the place. What I saw through the lens looked sort of like a postcard from England: a thatched-roof cottage in a quiet English village, like the birthplace of a famous poet—say, maybe Thompson.

Just as I snapped the shutter, the sun divided into a thousand shafts streaming downward through the clouds, and a cottontail rabbit that had been enjoying a breakfast of red clover stood up on his hind legs and looked straight at me.

Perfect! I thought.

I used the rest of the roll on close-ups of ladybugs, yellow ones and orange ones, plus spiders, butterflies, and paint peeling from an old shed door.

I also tried to get a picture of a deer at the edge of the woods, but I think he was too far away. Still, my artistic confidence was higher, I paid closer attention to the light conditions, and I thought one or two of my shots might turn out to be keepers.

When I placed the roll in the yellow postpaid envelope to send to Sparkle Snapshot in St. Louis, I thought about paying two dollars extra to get double prints but finally decided against it because at this time in our lives two dollars is two dollars.

However, something was changing in the way I looked at things. In the days of waiting for my film to get to the lab and for the lab to do whatever it is they do when they get it and for the United States Postal Service to get it back to me, I must have seen a hundred excellent picture opportunities.

Wouldn't it be nice to be rich enough to take a picture of everything that catches your eye?

Wouldn't it be nice to freeze all the beauty that crosses your path?

Man, that would be something!

I'll do that right after I build a library for Paisley.

Chief Leopard Frog says eventually you learn to do it with your mind's eye, but I find that my mind's eye's brain has a tendency to forget. That's when pictures become extraordinarily helpful.

Leaning against a cottonwood tree, the official tree of the state of Kansas, I pondered this thought.

Here's what I came up with:

Just as a hammer is a tool for increasing force against the head of a nail, the camera is a tool for the extension of memory.

I was pretty proud of this insight.

But, of course, there was nobody to share it with.

My thoughts are trees falling in silence in an empty forest.

Wildlife Photography

IT WAS ALMOST SEPTEMBER. Most kids in Kansas were going back to school, but my mother surprised me one afternoon after *Oprah* by saying that due to our geographical circumstances, I would not be among them.

"I've signed you up for homeschool," she announced. "The nearest public school is simply too far away. You'd be riding a bus in darkness over bad roads twice a day. It's too much of a risk, not to mention a hardship. I, for one, do not want to be making bologna sandwiches at four o'clock in the morning."

"But Mom," I said, "how will I ever meet anybody my own age? It's like we're living on an ice shelf near the South Pole. Except we don't even have penguins."

"I'm sorry," she replied. "It's the best we can do right now. Maybe next year our lives will change."

When my pictures came back from St. Louis, I went to my room to open the package.

There was one shot of a spider eating a moth that was extraordinary. The light was perfect. The spider looked terrifying. The moth appeared to be a tiny rag of dust and parts.

The picture of the deer was a blur. The peeling paint could have been an abstract painting hanging in a big city museum. But it was the portrait of Ma Puttering's cottage that made me gasp, for there, in the foreground, was Ma Puttering herself, using a long-handled hoe to chop weeds in her squash garden.

This is no mistake at the lab, I realized.

This was something much, much bigger.

They say that people who are confined to prison cells or hospital rooms look forward most of all to meals and mail. At least, the optimistic ones do. Even when the postal service brings nothing and the food is cold, boring, and undercooked, there's always tomorrow.

As the last kid in Paisley, Kansas, I felt a lot in common with the incarcerated. Solitary confinement versus solitary freedom. What's the difference? Either way, your world is very small.

In part because of the danger involved, I decided to shoot an entire roll of film on bees.

The pumpkin flowers attracted several varieties, I noticed: honeybees, bumblebees, and several other kinds of very small bees that one could easily mistake for flies.

The technical challenges proved greater than I'd imagined. To get a good macro photo you have to be within a couple of inches of your subject. You also have to shoot at a slower shutter speed than normal, which means your subject can't be moving.

Try telling that to a bee!

As with all worthwhile endeavors, my work required patience.

"Look at it this way," Chief Leopard Frog said. "If you were fishing, you might sit for hours before you got a bite."

"True," I replied.

"Anyway, what's the rush?" he added, using a phrase that was well on its way to becoming my personal motto.

In the morning hours, in late summer, a pumpkin patch is a very busy place. The broad leaves of the pumpkin plant are bigger than the hands of a man, and the vines twist and turn and angle themselves to capture sunlight.

Underneath, even on the hottest days, is a cool jungle floor teeming with life. Toads hide here, as do mice, lizards, and skinks, and because they're here, snakes come. Crawling insects, arachnids, caterpillars, worms, and once in a while a rabbit all move quietly beneath the floppy leaves.

Above is an insect airport with takeoffs and landings going on constantly.

I sat on a wooden crate and staked out a flower that was close enough for me to lean in to when the time came.

Patience, I told myself.

What's the rush?

Twenty-four exposures on a single strip of celluloid film. One pumpkin flower. Hundreds of bees. And all the time in the world.

Actually, that last statement is more of a euphemism, or perhaps an attitude, than a statement of fact. Pumpkin flowers prefer early sunlight.

By ten o'clock in the morning, they begin to close, folding their star-shaped petals into an impenetrable yellow cone. At that time, the bees are forced to search elsewhere, perhaps to seek out honeysuckle or clover.

On the first day, I made three shots, of which one—I was hopeful—captured the image of a pollen-covered bumblebee.

After that, all I had to look forward to was the mail and lunch, neither of which proved to be particularly eventful.

I spent an entire week on bees. I got portraits of seven different bees of three different varieties. Now, of course, I wanted to learn more about bees. It's one thing to know what they look like— alien creatures with huge compartmentalized eyes—but it's quite another to know what they do.

But there is no library in Paisley.

I did get stung once, right on the tip of my right thumb, which hurt like the dickens and made my thumb swell up to twice its normal size.

"You're obviously allergic to bee stings, Spencer," my mother said, wrapping my thumb in a cool compress and giving me an antihistamine to ease the pain. "I don't want you playing with them anymore."

"I wasn't playing," I explained.

A Very Special Camera

A WEEK ISN'T LONG to wait for something. Not even for Christmas. Two weeks, however, is a different story. Two weeks is a long way away. In the olden days, they called two weeks a fortnight, a word that suggests that somehow you have to get past the well-guarded fort to arrive at the night you've been dreaming of.

A fortnight.

If you were to order something and had to wait a fortnight, chances are you would soon stop thinking about it and begin fretting over something else. Consequently, when at last it showed up it would be a surprise.

"Oh!" you would say. "Look what came today!"

As if you had had nothing to do with it.

Like a dog burying a bone so later he can "discover" it.

"Hey," he says to himself. "What luck!"

Green pumpkins the size of baseballs had formed in the shadows beneath the vines when my pictures finally arrived from Sparkle Snapshot in St. Louis.

I had forgotten about the wasp portrait. My, but he was an evil-looking fellow. A poison dart with a grudge is what he was—a wriggling, saber-shaped creature with a stinger at the end of his

35

abdomen that could puncture your skin more efficiently than a med tech's hypodermic needle.

I placed that snapshot aside, expecting next to see perhaps the eyeball of a honeybee. Instead, I found myself staring into the face of my father.

You could have knocked me over with dog dander!

I knew it had to be him, even though I'd never met him. I'd seen pictures my mother had kept, and besides, he was wearing the peach-colored Columbus Catfish baseball cap that I had on my head right now. Moreover, he kind of looked like me, or, more accurately, I was beginning to look like him.

There were two snapshots of him in the pack of twenty-four nature portraits, each quite similar, as if taken only seconds apart. He was smiling, but self-consciously so, perhaps uncomfortable with having his picture taken, or possibly, I speculated, uncomfortable in the presence of bees.

I wouldn't blame him. My thumb bears a scar from the attack I endured. It's a fine line less than half an inch long that cuts right through my fingerprint. It's strange to think that a bee can alter your fingerprint for all time.

It's strange to see one's father after so many years.

Surprise!

It soon became apparent that my mother's concept of home-schooling was for me to stay home from school while she did her paperwork and watched TV. Apparently, if any schooling was to take place, I would have to school myself.

Since I'd hit a dead end on my investigation of bees, I decided to concentrate on finding a logical explanation for people from my past appearing at random among my photographs.

Someone at Sparkle Snapshot was deliberately enclosing these pictures for me, or there was supernatural interference taking place during the fortnight's journey to and/or from St. Louis.

Tampering with the U.S. mail is a serious offense, whether performed by the living or the dead.

I mentioned this to Chief Leopard Frog. He seemed unfazed.

"Not everything has a logical explanation," Chief Leopard Frog advised. "Some things just happen."

"The only reason some things have no logical explanation," I argued, "is because we haven't figured out the answers yet."

"You are an optimistic boy," Chief Leopard Frog observed.

I began my investigation with an examination of the negatives.

Negatives are returned to the customer packaged with the positive prints—the snapshots. They are cut into consecutively numbered strips consisting of five images each.

If the mystery pictures had corresponding negatives, I reasoned, that would suggest that the photos came from my camera. If not, then it would mean that somebody—or something—had deliberately mixed the ghost pictures in with my order.

I held the first strip up to the light and squinted.

Negatives for color print film are ruby-colored with darks and lights reversed, so it's a world of distorted perception that takes getting used to.

Still, there she was, in a neat rectangle right next to a giant caterpillar with a single horn, my ex-neighbor, the attractive, flirtatious older teen, Maureen Balderson.

In the next packet, I found Ma Puttering adjacent to a ladybug, its pale spots as big as Chief Leopard Frog's namesake's namesake.

The clincher was in the third packet: two pictures of my ghost father, side by side, sharing a five-image strip of red celluloid with a bumblebee, a sweat bee, and a wasp.

Not only had these images been exposed using my camera, but they had been exposed during the time that I was taking the other pictures.

Where is the logical explanation for that?

"Look at it this way," Chief Leopard Frog suggested. "At least you've ruled out your mother as a suspect."

"I didn't know she was a suspect," I said.

"Good heavens, Spencer," Chief Leopard Frog responded. "She handles every piece of mail coming in and out of Paisley. Of course she was a suspect."

The Last Kid in Paisley, Kansas

YOU MAY THINK that I was bored, but this was not the case. You may reasonably suspect that I was lonely, but except for wishing for a dog, I wasn't.

Not particularly.

I did find everyday life to be a strange experience, like being shipwrecked, or left behind on the moon when the last spacecraft departs for earth, but I kept myself busy, walking through the fields and observing all the subtle changes as summer gave up its last great blast of hot air while the animals who knew the drill were preparing for the hard times to come.

Winter on the prairie is like death.

Autumn, which can be gorgeous, is no time to stop and smell the sunflowers. For those in the know, it's the busy season.

I wondered about the kids at school.

Were they having lunch now? Were they cutting up and carrying on and laughing? What kind of shoes was everybody wearing this year? Last year, it was black basketball shoes. This year was bound to be different.

I think my mother has never gotten over the loss of my father.

I think that's why she sits around and watches TV.

I took a picture of a baby pumpkin. It looked like an acorn, except it was much bigger and green. There is no logical explanation for how a single pumpkin seed becomes a jungle littered with fat, heavy orange orbs.

Oh, I know that scientists say they've figured it out. I know about photosynthesis, and cell division, and all of that. But really now. One little seed the size of a fingernail becomes a huge, wild thicket of ropelike vines? Orange, basketball-size fruits that contain ten thousand or more copies of the seed that started them?

A scientific explanation, perhaps.

But logical?

I think not.

Perhaps, I reasoned, there is some connection between my camera and my dreams.

My dreams are populated with people from Paisley. Neighbors, shopkeepers, teachers, kids, bus drivers, waitresses, pizza deliverymen—even babies and dogs. Over the course of time, they all show up in my dreams.

In my dreams, Paisley lives.

The camera, too, is a way to hold on to the past, in a fragmentary, visual, dreamlike way. More than extension of memory, as I had previously observed.

A giver of life.

Could the logical explanation have something to do with this?

I'm not lonely. But sometimes after I dream about a particular person or event, I wake up crying.

I wish I could tell someone.

I wish I could step back into the dream and keep it going.

I wish I didn't have to let go of everything I've ever known.

Chief Leopard Frog was only part right. I needed something to do not only with my hands.

I needed something to do with my thoughts.

Tremendous thunderstorms rolled through one night, the kind that explode like mortar shells, tilt pictures on the wall, and rattle windows. By morning, the prairie was as squishy as a bathroom sponge and the pumpkin patch looked like the creature from the haunted lagoon, its dangling ringlet tendrils grasping for the paint-chipped windows of the house.

Leaping expertly from a single silk tightrope, a spider as fat as a California grape ducked behind a leaf when it saw me coming with my camera. Filtered through gauzy cloud cover and illuminating a newly refreshed world, the sunlight itself was green, causing Paisley to glow like the Emerald City.

My destination this time was Crossroads Circle.

According to a stapled-together sixteen-page pamphlet from the Franks collection, published by D. Potts Small Town Histories, Davenport, Iowa, Crossroads Circle in Paisley was once a busy intersection of two rural highways, with an elevated walled circle in the center in which was planted a colorful garden of pansies, or zinnias, or mums, depending on the season, and from which rose a flagpole bearing the proud if somewhat overdesigned banner of the United States of America.

"Stars AND stripes?" the anonymous author had opined. "One or the other, but not both."

Because most people don't expect to encounter a traffic roundabout way out in the country, virtually every vehicular accident that ever happened in Paisley happened here, including a single-vehicle crash involving a street sweeper.

Once upon a time, it was a busy place.

Around the circle, shops congregated shoulder to shoulder, harmoniously, like dairy cattle gathered around a feeding station.

Some shopkeepers sold fresh meat. Some sold homemade candy. Some sold goat's milk soap. Some, as I've mentioned, such as Mrs. Franks, sold books.

One place that I remember myself sold original yard art created from rusted farm implements and kitchen utensils. My favorite was the armadillo family made from airtight Tupperware bowls.

Crossroads Circle was the heart of Paisley, where the people whose front yards were measured not in feet but in acres came to spend a little time with people like themselves—or not, as the case may be.

Mankind wasn't meant to live alone.

God had that figured out right after he created Adam.

Spencer Adams Honesty.

The last kid in Paisley, Kansas.

The Sad History of Paisley, Kansas

Part One

IN MY SHORT LIFETIME, T. J. Heath's General Merchandise Emporium was one of the first stores in Paisley to give up the ghost.

Mr. Heath sold everything. Hardware. Clothes. Lip gloss. Jams and jellies. Livestock water troughs. Skunk repellent. Deer jerky. Udder balm.

Everybody went to Mr. Heath's store because Mr. Heath had something for everybody. But one day, a couple of months after the Paisley plastics plant closed and the Wal-Mart Supercenter over in Coy opened up with a ribbon-cutting ceremony presided over by the lieutenant governor and his pretty third wife, Mr. Heath spent an entire day without a single customer.

Disgusted, he went out back to his little lumberyard and got some boards and nailed up all the doors and windows, never to return. The stuff that was on the shelves he just left there, where, over time, the once valuable inventory was inherited by moths and mice and rust, and, of course, the ever-present spiders.

I peeked through gaps in the boards. A foul scent of rodent droppings, decay, and mildew wafted through the cracks. Inside were bags of seed and cornstarch and flour that had rotted apart or been torn open by vermin, the contents scattered like muddy puppy paws across Mr. Heath's once spotless, highly polished hardwood floors.

Clothes that had been hung neatly on plastic hangers now dangled precariously from the remnants of rotted seams. Bottles of soda and syrup and cooking oil had fallen to the floor and broken, combining to form a tiny tar pit in which a thousand flies had lost their troubled lives.

Labels had disappeared from cans. Small appliances, such as toasters and waffle irons, had succumbed to tarnish and rust; home electronics, once the latest thing, had passed into obsolescence.

The scene before me might have been a museum, a snapshot in time, a three-dimensional picture of Paisley's past, except that in its present condition it more closely resembled a shipwreck, as I would imagine the interior of the doomed *Titanic* at the bottom of the sea.

A shopwreck with no survivors.

I positioned my lens between two hammered-up boards, carefully sighted through the viewfinder, made note of the sunlight streaming through a hole in the roof, adjusted my exposure accordingly, set my legs apart to form a human bipod, and snapped the shutter.

Some, who live in cities, with vast forces of police, and homes and businesses protected by alarm systems, and surveillance cameras, and guard dogs, may wonder why no one has ever broken in to Mr. Heath's abandoned store.

The answer is uniquely Paisley. First, it was because the people who lived here, all of whom knew one another by sight, were basically honest. After that, it was because no one lived here at all.

Can a thief break in if there are no thieves around?

Before Kansas was Kansas, there were no towns, but there were plenty of people. Today these people are called Native Americans and few of them are left.

Before I began being homeschooled—that is, left to figure out things for myself—I learned from my teachers that during the days of the European settlement of America these people were called Indians.

Indians were largely treated as inconvenient savages whose presence impeded progress.

European settlers brought with them the idea that land was something a person could own. This was contrary to the Indians' point of view. They believed that the land, like the air and the rain and the sun and the stars, belonged to everybody.

With the notion of ownership of land came the idea of towns, each staked out into adjacent rectangles with "lots" for sale or for claim to those who would "improve" them by building structures— houses, businesses, and factories.

Encouraged by the United States government, people came from all over the eastern United States, and parts of western Europe, Scandinavia, and even eastern Europe to "tame" the Kansas territory.

Many people became rich convincing others who were less informed to come to Kansas to settle a town. Many other people died broke and brokenhearted trying to do just that.

Consequently, in the nineteenth century, hundreds of towns in Kansas came and went.

Today there are places that are simply ruts in a pasture that once were home to hundreds, even thousands, of optimistic Scandinavians and Germans.

Two of the most influential factors in determining whether a town would prosper or wither were the owners of the railroads and the politicians who determined the locations of the county seats, the various headquarters for local government.

Corruption among these people was rife.

Heck, they didn't even consider their underhanded shenanigans to be corrupt. They saw themselves as being savvy enough to outsmart the next guy, a desirable American trait.

In the D. Potts pamphlet about Paisley, the author rages about these dishonest practices, terming them "unchecked hucksterism."

I just call it human nature.

The Sad History of Paisley, Kansas

Part Two

LUCK HAS A LOT TO DO WITH the success of a town. But so do the schemes of strangers.

For example, if the railroad decided to build a station in your new town, business would boom and your town would grow rapidly. If the railroad decided to lay its tracks five miles away, for whatever reason—carelessness, stupidity, or most often some form of kickback or bribery—your town was doomed.

Similarly, if the elected officials in the state government decided that your town should house all the county records and contain the county courthouse, your town would be a magnet for visitors for all the years to come, and would thrive.

If these politicians decided against your town and chose another, where perhaps they themselves had made investments, your town's luck had just run out.

Add to these capricious man-made threats the fierce climate of the prairie, which has been known to wipe out entire communities with grass fires, tornadoes, or drought, or clobber thousands of head of cattle at a single blow with a sudden, blinding blizzard, and you can see that there is nothing especially permanent about a Kansas town, which the Indians, a race of experienced people who followed opportunity as opportunity shifted, knew all too well.

"Owning land," Chief Leopard Frog once told me, "is like owning time. It is an exercise in folly."

The influence of the railroads waned with the construction of highways. Now the deciding factor became whether the highway would pass through your town. Again, the decision was left to politicians in a distant city. The people who lived in the town were at the mercy of other people who had no reason to show mercy. Your town was nothing more than a speck on a map. Specks don't matter much.

Money does.

After that, it was the factories. As one by one the farms failed, the factories took up the slack, providing jobs for the men and women who previously had worked the fields. Then the companies that owned the factories learned that they could make more money by moving their factories to other countries where people were even more desperate than the people in your town.

And so again, one by one, factories closed and the people in the town were left with nothing.

Many struggled to maintain their lives as they thought their lives were meant to be, farming, fixing broken farm machinery, and carving irregular-shaped bowls from walnut trees. But without steady economic nourishment, the towns eventually died and disappeared.

Those who could moved to bigger towns, or, if they had a large enough grubstake, to the cities.

Those who could not grew pumpkins and watched TV.

In the meantime, the buffalo had all been killed, the prairie grasses plowed under, the Indians displaced or, more often, exterminated by European diseases, and the early settlers had gone scrambling off to Colorado and California in search of gold.

It was into this environment that Paisley was born—and much

later, myself—with nothing much going for it other than cheap land and high hopes.

The founder and first mayor of Paisley was a man named Daschell Potts.

Daschell Potts was a mysterious figure, having come out of nowhere and, later, having returned to the same place. But what he had going for him was a wardrobe of tailored white suits and crisp Panama hats. He wore a black string tie and fancied himself to be a Kentucky colonel, although he seemed more a caricature than the real thing.

He told people that he had once written a book, although Mrs. Franks, the former bookstore owner and a well-read woman in her own right, said she had never heard of him.

The selection of the name Paisley is worthy of mention. Apparently a group of city leaders met and during the discussion got into an argument about whether to name the town Red, Green, Blue, or Yellow, as each had a particular reason for favoring a certain color signifying something such as a wheat field, a sunrise, the big sky, or a verdant crop.

After several rounds of indecisive voting and more rounds of quality Kentucky bourbon supplied by the well-heeled Colonel Potts, they compromised on the name Paisley, representing a combination of colors, and that was that.

Now that I think about it, I guess I came within a hair's breadth of being born in a town called Plaid.

The plastic novelty factory was the engine that ran the town for many years. Not surprisingly, it was owned in part by Colonel Potts.

Colonel Potts was generous when it came to the support of the town. He built the elementary school, the middle school, the high school, the bandstand, and the ballpark.

Once each year he sponsored the Paisley Olympics, which consisted of sack races, three-legged races, diving contests at Paisley Lake, and a stock car race that took place on Highway LL, to the calculated innocence of state authorities. There was also the equivalent of a state fair for domesticated animals. Best cow, best sheep, best chicken, and best rabbit—all were eligible for cash prizes from the deep pockets of Colonel Potts.

Then the factory was sold to some bored foreign visitors and closed for good in Paisley, and the party was over.

Colonel Potts simply vanished.

The town soon followed.

Luck Happens

ON A SECOND-FLOOR windowsill of Mr. Heath's store I spied what appeared to be a hummingbird nest.

What a great opportunity for macro photos! I thought.

Perhaps there would be eggs in the nest. Possibly even baby hummingbirds. Although it was late in the season for babies of any species, I figured it was worth a look. I had never seen a baby hummingbird, much less photographed one.

Luckily, the random hammering of the hotheaded Mr. Heath had created what amounted to a climbing wall. With my camera slung around my neck, I gripped one board with my hands while placing the toe of my tennis shoe on a board below. If I was careful, it would be an easy task.

Of course, what I hadn't given any thought to was the condition of Mr. Heath's handiwork. You know how people like to say "Time heals all things"? Well, those people are basically stupid. Because what happens is exactly the opposite:

Time rots all things.

The visible decay inside Mr. Heath's establishment should have warned me what to expect on the outside. Untreated pine lumber hastily affixed to a vertical surface has a useful life as brief as a monarch butterfly's.

When the board separated in my hands some fifteen feet above the ground, I fell backwards onto a tumbledown pile of concrete blocks, striking the back of my head and snapping my left clavicle—my collarbone—clean in two. Something was also wrong with my left leg.

If a boy falls in a ghost town when no one is around, does he make a sound?

Of all the dumb things that people say to one another, here, I think, is the dumbest. Following a catastrophe in which you have nearly been killed, the people who previously were walking around saying "Time heals all things" now are prone to say "Boy, were you lucky."

The doctor who treated me actually said this the following afternoon after I'd spent the night lying on the ground in excruciating pain, getting bitten by mosquitoes and crawled on by whatever sorts of bugs and slimy creatures perform their errands at night.

"It's a good thing you were wearing that orange cap, else your mother might never have found you," Dr. Appletree said. "It was like a bright signal by the side of the road."

First of all, my father's Columbus Catfish cap is peach, not orange. Second, there is nothing lucky about falling and breaking your bones. Third, I might add, and would have done so right then and there if Dr. Appletree had not been attempting to maneuver my severed collarbone into a position allowing it to be held in place with a sling, a profoundly painful experience, where is the luck in living in a ghost town where nobody even comes looking for you until nearly twenty-four hours after you've gone missing?

The only lucky part about the entire experience, so far as I was concerned, was that my camera survived the fall.

My collarbone would take weeks to heal. The back of my head

had a goose egg literally as big as a goose egg, and my left leg was bruised and swollen as if it'd received a thousand bee stings.

It would not have surprised me if the goofball Dr. Appletree had said, "It's a lucky thing that you don't go to school, Spencer, because now you can't."

Luck.

Who are these people who try to make bad luck sound like it's good luck?

My guess is that they're some of the world's luckiest people.

That lucky Dr. Appletree's clinic was across the street from Wal-Mart. He had no competitors and could charge his patients as much money as he liked.

My world became as small as it had been at my birth, consisting of my bedroom and nothing more. I couldn't use crutches because my broken collarbone couldn't take the weight. I couldn't use my left arm because it was strapped into a sling. Everything I had taken for granted had been compromised. Turning the pages of a book. Taking pictures. Eating with a fork. Going to the bathroom. It was all an ordeal requiring planning and patience.

I took pills for the pain and slept a lot.

Once again, time had become distorted.

That first day home, when I woke up, it was dark, the television in the next room was silent, and Chief Leopard Frog was sitting quietly in the rocking chair opposite my bed.

"What are you staring at?" I asked, not bothering to disguise the hostility in my voice.

"Just watching over you," he replied.

"Ha!" I retorted. "That's a laugh! Where were you when I fell from the side of the store? Where were you when I lay dying in the weeds? Where were you when the insects decided that I was a sacred feast sent to them from the Bug God? And if I remember correctly, wasn't it you who suggested that I should give up my former idleness and begin to use my hands? Look where *that's* gotten me!"

"It's good to see that there's nothing wrong with your brain," Chief Leopard Frog responded. "Your expressions of anger are perfectly normal. Within a few weeks, except for an unfortunate lump, your collarbone will be, too."

"If you say so," I replied. "In the meantime, I have to hop on one leg to go pee and am confined to live in a world no bigger than a Christmas snow globe."

"And you're suggesting that's a bad thing?" Chief Leopard Frog asked. "Wait to find out. After all, what's the rush?"

An Artist in a Cage

"There's nothing to do," I complained to Chief Leopard Frog. "I've passed the point of absolute boredom into the zone of terminal boredom."

"Good, good, all good," Chief Leopard Frog counseled. "Now we can work on patience."

Back in the days of the famous French Impressionists and Fauvists, those daring, bohemian painters in Paris in the late nineteenth and early twentieth centuries who shocked the world with their new, liberated view of color and shape and subject, it was not unusual to find entire paintings devoted to an artist's chair, or his bed, or his window, or his lunch, or his table.

Indeed, according to the Disney comic book *Uncle Scrooge on Art, Music, and Money,* today such images are highly prized and hang in the world's finest collections and museums. Some, such as a yellow chair by Van Gogh, or a red tablecloth by Matisse, are worth millions and millions of dollars.

Why such a fuss over such ordinary subjects?

I can tell you.

Those guys were stuck in their rooms.

What else was there to look at?

They had no money to go anywhere, and if they did manage to scrape up a few francs to go somewhere it was most likely downstairs to the café to meet girls, where their money was quickly gone.

Better to spend a few days painting a likeness of the chest of drawers, however wobbly and unlikely the end result.

For the first time in my life I understood these paintings, although, of course, being a native of Paisley, Kansas, I'd never actually seen them. But I'd seen reproductions in several of the better books deeded to me by Mrs. Franks.

Now I was also a room-bound artist.

My paintbrush was a somewhat antiquated thirty-five-millimeter camera. My world was a bedroom measuring approximately twelve by fourteen feet. I did have one advantage over those tortured Frenchmen. I had a macro lens. If it suited me, I could photograph my bedspread close enough to see the hand-woven fibers crisscrossing like the ties on tiny railroad tracks.

My first exposure under my new circumstances was a fly that had parked himself on the top of my bookcase. Instead of swatting him with my mother's *TV Guide*, which I probably should have done, thereby dealing with two nuisances at once, I took his picture as he scratched his hairy legs. Only the *click-thunk* of the shutter scared him off.

Country flies are bold creatures.

Whereas Van Gogh concentrated on the entire piece of rough-hewn furniture in his habitat, I focused on the knobs, the grain of the wood, the imperfections in the paint.

A loose screw in a hinge became a visual metaphor for all that was wrong with my life. A dripping faucet in the bathroom was an opportunity to express the relentless passing of time. Rust stains around the bathtub drain spoke to me of age and futility. A casually discarded T-shirt, lying like a carcass on the floor, stood for the meaninglessness of personal attachments, the fragility of human bonds.

I was an artist in a cage.

Of course, I had no visitors.

Other than Chief Leopard Frog, who came and went as the mood struck him, and the occasional prison-guard visit from my mother, delivering food, I was utterly, entirely alone.

It didn't take long for me to learn that two pain pills would help to pass the time better than one, and three could get me through an afternoon.

I began to complain of increasing pain simply to get more pills.

No one questioned my motives.

And why should they? They perceived their lives, though empty, to be very busy. They'd move from one interruption of their idle thoughts to the next. Who cares if there's a kid out in the country somewhere who's getting more medication than he needs?

Certainly not the overworked (and overpaid) Dr. Appletree.

Certainly not the ever-changing pharmacists at Wal-Mart.

That I spent my days in a drug-induced stupor is adequately demonstrated in the several out-of-focus pictures that came back to me in the mail a fortnight later.

But the interior of T. J. Heath's General Merchandise Emporium was a prizewinner, if I do say so myself. The story that it told in an instant was profound. Most of the others in the collection were throwaways. Blurry coat hangers holding nothing. Boring bedposts. A toilet at the moment of flush. My talisman sitting on a windowsill.

That sort of thing.

But as had become the custom, there was a ghost in the mix

from Sparkle Snapshot. This time the ghost was Mr. Heath. He was out in his lumberyard, gathering pieces of pine boards that had fallen from his handmade storage rack. He had a pained expression on his face.

Just before I passed out from all those pills, an idea began to form in my foggy mind.

Saved by the Mail

WHAT IF, I wondered, *I used the ghost camera to photograph all the people of Paisley?*

I mulled the idea over in my mind. This was not easy, since I had taken four pain pills at once and soon passed out again for hours.

A hurricane was approaching the heavily populated South Florida coast. An unexpected blizzard stranded hundreds of motorists in the Rockies. On the other side of the world, entire villages floated away after days of heavy rains. Wars were raging in the Middle East, Africa, and Asia.

I was oblivious to all of this. My world was no longer the abandoned town of Paisley. It wasn't even my own room. By abusing the pain pills that had been allocated to me by people who otherwise had washed their hands of my situation, I had reduced my world to a few simple sensations in my brain.

I had finally succeeded in locating the macro within me.

What a shame I couldn't take its picture.

Something had to change.

Is it against the law to take a catalog with someone else's name on it even when you know that person couldn't care less whether he ever gets the catalog? Or is this one of those "technicalities"—

that is, something that clearly is against the law but nobody gives a rat's patoot about it so why bring it up?

I wouldn't want my mother to lose her phony-baloney job over my possibly criminal actions, but most of this stuff was just going into the recycling bin anyway.

I began to help myself to the undeliverable catalogs that came in each day to the Paisley post office—i.e., my house. It was the only fresh reading material I had.

Among the subjects I was introduced to during my long convalescence were fishhooks, imported cigars, Japanese skin care products, Maine woolen outerwear, discount office supplies, and Dutch bulb gardens.

Some catalogs specialized in gift items, absolutely useless things that you could never use yourself but might be fun to palm off on others. My favorite was a miniature working catapult that fired diminutive farm animals across the room. If I'd had forty dollars to spare, I would have ordered it. As it was, I had no extra money. Every penny was earmarked for my photographic endeavors.

There is little difference between living in a ghost town and living in a dream world.

The pet care catalogs gave me real pause.

If only I had a dog, I thought, *I wouldn't have to depend on this imaginary Indian who comes and goes like a will-o'-the-wisp, dispensing dubious advice.*

The weirdest catalog I came across was one for sex toys. It was so strange that it made me never want to grow up. I shuddered as I shoved it to the bottom of a trash bag.

If this is the future, I thought, *what's the rush?*

My bed, which is where I was spending ninety-nine percent of my time, was no longer a conventional human's bed. As my needs had changed, I'd converted it into something resembling a great blue heron's nest, piling up comforters and pillows into a concave, circular shape and positioning myself in the middle.

There was no cozier place to ride out a thunderstorm.

"I'm concerned about what's happening to you," my mother said one afternoon during a long commercial about plastic food storage devices that for some reason put me in mind of armadillos. "Don't you think you should try to walk around a little bit?"

"If I could, I would," I told her emphatically. "But I can't."

As fate had planned it, the very next day the catalog pile produced a curious little brochure printed in black-and-white on cheap newsprint called *Uncle Milton's Thousand Things You Thought You'd Never Find.*

A manual chicken beak blunter was something I'd never thought about finding, but if I had thought about a manual chicken beak blunter, I bet I would have found one somewhere, so Uncle Milton may have been overpromising, but that's salesmanship. Anyway, it was an interesting collection and I skipped my next round of pills so I wouldn't fall asleep while reading it.

One device was a doorstop made to resemble a dead rat. It was quite realistic. Uncle Milton certainly had me on that one, because I couldn't possibly imagine there being a market for such a thing, especially at twenty-nine ninety-five, plus shipping.

Other novelties were truly one of a kind, such as the 3D glasses for dogs ("guaranteed to work or you should get a different dog") and the miracle spray solution that would repel mosquitoes, stop rust, and attract fish all at the same time ("a must for the serious fisherman").

There was an upside-down chair that I seriously considered ordering. You attach it to your ceiling with its supersuction feet and invite your guests to make themselves comfortable. ("A million laughs," Uncle Milton promised.)

But it was the item in the upper-right-hand corner on page thirty-two that really got my attention. Not the full-length whoopee cushion that fits under an entire row of outdoor bleachers such as you might find at a minor-league baseball game, but the one next to it:

"Ghost Camera Takes Pictures of the Past," Uncle Milton's caption read. "This is no ordinary time-lapse camera. This is a real, working time machine. Uses ordinary film to capture images from both the recent and the distant past. Non-programmable. Batteries not included. Use at your own risk."

What risk? I wondered.

Hands Across the Sea

How much money something is worth depends largely on how much money you have.

At four hundred and ninety-five dollars and ninety-five cents plus insurance and shipping for a ghost camera, Uncle Milton might as well have been offering to sell an authentic orbiting space satellite. There was no way I could ever buy it. But since I already had a camera that seemed to possess some of the same characteristics as his camera, I wondered if a letter to Uncle Milton asking about his experience with such matters might be in order.

I skipped my next round of pain pills in order to compose a letter that struck just the right tone.

Perhaps, I thought, *if I also enclose an unusual item as a gift, he'll be more inclined to cooperate.*

But what?

A board from a tumbledown building in Paisley?

Who'd want it?

A baby pumpkin?

Not very hard to find.

My talisman! Definitely one of a kind, and just the sort of half-art, half-magic item that Uncle Milton seemed to delight in.

Surely Chief Leopard Frog would understand.

According to the fine print at the bottom of the inside front cover, *Uncle Milton's Thousand Things You Thought You'd Never Find* is not an American publication but is, in fact, the product of an enterprise headquartered in the Cayman Islands.

Off the top of my head I was unable to picture just where the Cayman Islands might be, but I sensed that it was a far cry from Paisley, Kansas—or Davenport, Iowa, for that matter.

Perhaps if I weren't being homeschooled, I would know. But maybe not, for as I recall, geography is a delicate subject for public school Kansans, who if they learn too many facts about the world might be tempted to leave.

Uncle Milton's Thousand Things You Thought You'd Never Find was edited by Milton A. Swartzman, Jr., who gave as his address P.O. Box 1991 GT, Grand Cayman, the Cayman Islands. There was no Zip Code or even a hint of what country might be involved in overseeing Mr. Swartzman's activities.

Apparently in his search for things you'd never expect to find, he was as free as a bird.

Dear Mr. Swartzman, I began.

I am a great admirer of your catalog of useful and unusual objects. It must have taken you a long time to assemble such a magnificent collection. As a token of my esteem, I enclose a hand-carved talisman from an authentic though admittedly imaginary Kansas Indian chief. It is reputed to bring luck to the bearer, and as I lie here in my nest of quilts with my broken collarbone and swollen leg and the back of my head lumped out like a Colorado boulder, I can certainly attest to its powers. It was my own medical doctor, a man named Dr. Appletree, who told me how lucky I was. Imagine how things might have turned out if I hadn't possessed the talisman!

And yet, I offer it to you in exchange for information.

Specifically, I refer to the ghost camera that you advertise on page thirty-two of your most recent catalog, just opposite the grandstand whoopee cushion. I think I may possess a camera with similar features. I was hoping that you could explain how yours works and if you have sold many of them over the years and what your customers report about them.

Any information you can provide would be appreciated. Please note that I am a homeschooled, housebound Kansas teenager, many miles from the nearest living soul except my mother and becoming increasingly desperate about my plight. Thus, I must depend upon the kindness of people of achievement such as yourself in order to learn anything at all.

Thank you for your kind consideration.

Sincerely,

Spencer Adams Honesty

General Delivery

Paisley, Kansas 66085

P.S. If you don't want the talisman, feel free to send it back.

SAH

That night, instead of lying around my room, I hobbled into the kitchen and had dinner with my mother. While waiting for the entrée to be served, I took a close-up photo of a black-eyed pea.

A fortnight passed without incident. The pumpkins grew in size, variety, and number, as did the spiders that had appointed themselves to guard them.

One day, a letter arrived, not typically a noteworthy event at a post office, but this letter bore a stamp with a painting of a menacing-looking bearded pirate dressed in boots, pirate hat, leather breeches, and a gold-buttoned coat. In his right hand he was holding aloft a scimitar, raised toward a symbol of a crown and the official mark of the queen of England. In his left hand he pointed a blunderbuss toward the words CAYMAN ISLANDS.

In the background of this scene, a complex and colorful painting no bigger than a single exposure on a roll of film, two tough-looking brigands appeared to be burying (or digging up) a pirate chest, while near the horizon a pirate ship lay at anchor, above which was the designation 10c. Most surprising of all, the stamp was affixed to a letter addressed to me.

It's from Uncle Milton! I thought immediately.

Developing a Concept

"THIS IS SO COOL!" I exclaimed. "I actually got a letter from Uncle Milton!"

"Who's Uncle Milton?" Chief Leopard Frog wanted to know.

"He's just this guy," I replied. "A publisher."

"Poetry?" Chief Leopard Frog inquired.

"What?" I asked.

"Does he publish poetry?" Chief Leopard Frog repeated.

"I don't know," I answered. "Maybe."

"Well, if he does, I have a few verses I'd like to send him," Chief Leopard Frog said.

"Do you mind?" I said, annoyed. "I'm kind of busy here."

"I'll go find those poems," Chief Leopard Frog said.

"Good idea," I replied as he left the room.

Dear Kid, the letter began.

Please don't do me any more favors. I carried that so-called lucky talisman around for one day, which was all it took for me to fall into an open manhole and break my leg. And get this—the doctor who set it for me? He said, "You were really lucky this time." What a putz! Anyway, I passed your talisman on to some schmuck who deserves it more than you and I do. Can you guess who? Right. The bone doctor.

About the camera. I don't know much about it, to tell the truth, something I'm not particularly comfortable doing. I bought it from the widow of a witch doctor in Haiti a few years ago, along with a bunch of other stuff, like loaded human bone dice, a chicken-bone reproduction of the Eiffel Tower, the combination flyswatter-spatula (the Flatula®), and bomber jackets made from bats' wing membrane— I'm sure you saw them in the catalog. Neat stuff. Anyway, back to the camera: All I can tell you is that she said, "Never use it to take a picture of yourself." If you really want it, I can let you have it for 10 percent off retail, but you still have to pay shipping, insurance, etc.

Adios,

Milton Swartzman

President and Publisher, Uncle Milton's Thousand Things You Thought You'd Never Find.

Well!

You could have knocked me over with a spider!

This was the most interesting letter I had ever received. And so well written, too, with its disarmingly chatty style, cozy, informative, yet never losing sight of the need to sell. This Milton Swartzman had a gift, no doubt about it. Unfortunately, even with his generous discount, I still was in no position to purchase his camera, and neither was I ever likely to be, but the witch doctor's widow's warning he passed along about the operation of ghost cameras in general I would take to heart.

Why take chances?

Too bad about the talisman. I planned to ask Chief Leopard Frog to whittle me another one whenever he had time.

Meanwhile, I put the letter, the envelope, and, most important, the pirate postage stamp into the wooden cigar box where I'd begun to store my pictures.

I had some film left in the camera. I had run out of ideas about tiny things to photograph. The close-up perspective is interesting when you first see it, but art, I think, demands that the artist address grand themes.

For example, one spider, close up, may be a swell photo, but fifty different pictures of fifty different spiders, each composed with care and lit dramatically, and seen in its natural environment, well, that would be an artistic achievement.

Patience and effort.

You could do the same thing with, say, a dog's eyeballs, or out-of-state license plates, or the hair that grows from old men's ears and noses. You are limited only by your imagination. Unless, of course, you're stuck in an empty place called Paisley, Kansas, where there are no dogs, no old men, and no vehicles from anywhere, other than my mother's postal truck, which she drives with an expired license plate inasmuch as there is no law enforcement within miles.

That's when the idea returned to me. I'd photograph all the townspeople, every one, no matter how long it took. I'd stand in front of each house with the ghost camera, take a close-up or two of a doorknob or doorbell or house number, then stand back and shoot the whole house. Surely that would capture whatever essence the residents were percolating about.

I did the math.

When Paisley folded its tent, so to speak, there had been three hundred and fifteen full-time residents, not counting the part-time migrants who worked at the plant to help get ready for the Christmas season, or the proven idiots (methamphetamine manufacturers) who could hardly be designated as human.

There are twenty-four exposures on a roll of film. Let's say that with my amateur skill and general guesswork about ghost pictures

I could get eight former Paisleyans per roll, if I was lucky. That's three shots each, so I would need to buy forty rolls of film.

Wal-Mart sells thirty-five-millimeter film for less than two dollars a roll, so that would mean around eighty dollars for film and another, say, twenty for batteries, and then there would be the processing charges at Sparkle Snapshot, which had been running nearly five dollars a roll, so that's another two hundred bucks, easy.

Whew! I thought. *No wonder so many artists apply for government grants.*

Where would I get the money?

Deal with the Rich

MONEY! It's the grease for everything from art to business to space exploration.

The only thing of value I owned was my father's camera.

Disconsolate and discouraged, I set the lens for macro and aimlessly aimed my camera at my bare toe, the little one on the left foot, the one that curves to fit neatly into the row with the others, the one with only a tiny sliver of a toenail, the baby piggy that cried, "Wee, wee, wee," all the way home.

Or possibly it was "Oui, oui, oui."

One never knows the origins of those odd old stories.

Sighing, I examined the image before me with little interest and snapped the shutter.

Instantly, my toe disappeared.

Holy smokes! I thought, recalling the Haitian witch doctor's widow's warning: "Never use it to take a picture of yourself."

That lady wasn't kidding!

My financial dilemma remained unresolved for days. I continued to study the catalogs.

Who knew there were so many different kinds of stemware, vacuum cleaners, toilet seats, rubber bands, and chickens? You name it and there's somebody out there somewhere who's put together a catalog with a hundred variations on it.

One day, I was delighted to receive the latest edition of *Uncle Milton's Thousand Things You Thought You'd Never Find*. On page two it carried a two-line message inside a thick-bordered black box that read, "In Memoriam. Felix D. Katz, M.D."

Hmm, I thought. *Could Dr. Katz have been the one who got my lucky talisman?*

On page three was featured the Paisley-made joke-telling fish key chain that I'd gotten so long ago at Wal-Mart (for the price of a roll of film, I now realized!).

Uncle Milton's price was nine ninety-five.

That's a lot of money for a key chain, I thought.

That was when it dawned on me that Uncle Milton Swartzman must have a lot of money!

From there, the next thought was easy: *Write to Uncle Milton and ask him to underwrite my art project.*

Dear Mr. Swartzman, I wrote.

I'm so sorry to learn about your friend. Was it sudden? I hope he didn't suffer. Was it the lucky talisman?

The purpose of my letter is this: I am embarking on a major artistic undertaking involving the use of my own (presumed) ghost camera. I have calculated my expenses at three hundred dollars. Where I come from, that's a lot of money. I was wondering if you'd be willing to assist me. You are the only rich person I know. Otherwise, I wouldn't bother you. Actually, you are one of the few people I know, period, but that's another story.

Thanks for considering my request.

Sincerely,

Spencer Adams Honesty

P.S. Where are the Cayman Islands?

P.P.S. I enclose three poems written by my Indian friend. It wasn't my idea. He insisted.

Instead of having to wait a fortnight, I received Uncle Milton's reply at the end of the week, delivered right to my front door by FedEx. This in itself made for considerable excitement. Strangers rarely came to Paisley.

"I would have been here yesterday," the driver explained, "but I had trouble finding your town. Then, when finally I did find it, I took a look around and said, 'Criminy, what's the rush?'"

"Would you care to stay for dinner?" my mother asked. "It's fried chicken."

"I'd love to, ma'am," he said, "but I've got to get back to Kansas City to reload."

"I understand," my mother replied, disappointed.

Dear Kid, Milton Swartzman wrote:

I don't hand out money to anybody. It goes against all my principles, which are principally about my money. I will make you a deal, however. I will pay you five bucks apiece for as many of those bad luck amulets as you can talk your Indian pal into carving. They'll be a great addition to my catalog. That doctor had just stepped outside the hospital when a grand piano fell on him from five stories up. Splat! Just like that. Unfortunately, with my bad leg I was unable to recover the talisman. So you guys get busy and get me some more. You know, in a funny way, it's lucky you live in such a hard luck place. You could make some real dough.

Very truly yours,

Milton Swartzman

President and Publisher, Uncle Milton's Thousand Things You Thought You'd Never Find

P.S. The Cayman Islands are located in the Caribbean Sea between Cuba and Honduras.

P.P.S. Your friend carves knickknacks a lot better than he writes poetry.

P.P.P.S. The nurse came into my room to tell me about the doctor's accident and said, "In a way, he was very lucky."

"How's that?" I asked.

"Well," she replied, "it was a Steinway. That's the best there is."

I folded the letter carefully and slipped it back into the colorful FedEx cardboard envelope.

So here was the deal: By exporting Paisley's bad luck to the Cayman Islands one notched bee burl at a time, I could soon have the three hundred dollars I needed for my ambitious Paisley memorial photo-art project.

The big question now was how to convince Chief Leopard Frog to carve sixty more talismans. That's a pretty big order for an otherwise idle whittler.

Walking on Eggshells

I FOUND CHIEF LEOPARD FROG on the porch swing, feeding Cheetos to a squirrel.

"You're making his face orange," I observed.

"War paint," Chief Leopard Frog replied. "A great tradition."

"Okee-dokee," I said. "But it seems to me that it's not that much different from stirring up bees."

"It's completely different," Chief Leopard Frog replied.

Hmmm, I thought. *He seems to be somewhat miffed with me. Have I been neglecting him lately?*

Even when dealing with imaginary friends, it's important to be sensitive to their idiosyncrasies. So I started over, this time using a different approach, one based on the principles of salesmanship— flattery and lying—that, unknowingly, I'd begun to pick up from my contact with Milton Swartzman.

"Hey, guess what?" I said. "That publisher loved your poems."

"Really?" Chief Leopard Frog replied. His voice, his posture, and his demeanor suddenly brightened. "Which one did he like best?"

"He liked them all equally well," I fibbed. "He said there was no way to choose a favorite. He wants to see more."

"No kidding," Chief Leopard Frog said. "This is wonderful news."

"I hope you don't mind," I added, digging the hole deeper, "but I also let him see the talisman you made for me. He said you are truly a gifted artist capable of profound expression in many media."

"Wow," Chief Leopard Frog responded. "He said that?"

"Mmm-hmm," I replied.

"So what happens next?" Chief Leopard Frog inquired earnestly, dumping the entire bag of Cheetos at the feet of the squirrel, which was now covered in salty, cheese-flavored, iridescent orange dust.

Timing is everything. In photography. In fishing. In manipulating imaginary friends. You have to know when to set the hook.

"What do you mean, 'next'?" I asked disingenuously.

Chief Leopard Frog was always one for tradition. He spoke of tradition as if something that had happened in the past was more important—even sacred—just because it happened a long time ago. So I was simply following Chief Leopard Frog's ideas about tradition when I proceeded to deceive him for my own personal gain.

White men have been deceiving Native Americans for personal gain since the first greedy European set foot on this vast continent. The practice continues to this very day, as seen with all the gambling casinos in such unlikely places as Oklahoma and South Dakota. To my convenient way of thinking, there is no more long-standing tradition in the relationship between Indians and whites than relentless mutual exploitation.

Thus, my conscience shuddered only slightly when I said, "He wants to publish a book of your poems in conjunction with an exhibit of your art. He needs about sixty talismans and an equal number of poems. Can you do it?"

"It may take a while," Chief Leopard Frog replied. "But yes, of course I can."

"Way to go," I said encouragingly. "Let's get started right away, shall we?"

"I'll need some fresh notebooks," he said.

"Why don't we do the talismans first," I suggested. "We can always do a rush job later on the poems. How hard is it to write a poem?"

"Then I'll have to find another bee tree," Chief Leopard Frog explained. "That last one is about petered out."

"I'll help you," I replied. "Just follow the bees, right?"

One Sunday morning, back when there had been a First United Methodist Church of Paisley, the Reverend Dr. F. Foster Frost preached these words:

"Someday," he declared to his tiny congregation, a well-intentioned group that included my mother and myself, "God will demand that you pay for your sins."

In my experience, Dr. Frost was dead wrong. There's no "someday" about it. It's more like "within forty-five minutes. If you're really lucky, half a day."

Three hours after Chief Leopard Frog and I struck out in search of a new bee tree, I lay swollen and writhing in pain in my nest of quilts.

"Didn't I tell you that you're allergic to bee stings?" my mother shouted. "I'm beginning to wonder if you *can* be homeschooled. You're such a slow leaner."

"Ohhhh," I replied.

God's punishment is swift.

Meanwhile, however, Chief Leopard Frog sat outside on the front porch, whistling a happy tune as he whittled away like a happy-go-lucky dwarf in a Disney cartoon.

A Title That Couldn't Be Verse

NO SOONER WERE WE ALL AFLUTTER, what with poems and talismans, than Paisley, Kansas, was deflated like a hot-air balloon shot in its side by a vintage two-barrel shotgun.

Ka-ploop!

Things slowed down after that, and in Paisley, let me tell you, that's pretty doggone slow. Any slower and it would have been on a par with glacier formation or amber solidification.

I recovered from bee stings and broken bones and a bonked head while Chief Leopard Frog whittled and wrote poetry and whittled some more and my mother watched *Oprah* on TV and nobody but nobody came down our road, not even the FedEx man, who I had been certain would be back for my mother's fried chicken.

Pumpkins grew. Spiders crawled. My toe, the one I'd accidentally photographed into the fourth dimension, remained missing.

During this interlude I paused to reflect on the outrageous lie I had told my best friend. I was in a situation of my own making in which I could not defend my actions. That I was encouraged to do so by others, namely Milton Swartzman, only made it worse, because it proved me to be a moral weakling.

And yet I needed the money.

Isn't that what bank robbers say?

I was no better than a bank robber.

If it were not for the warning from the witch doctor's widow, I would have taken my own macro portrait.

That's how small I felt.

Like a bug.

Somehow, I was going to have to tell Chief Leopard Frog the truth.

Ohhhh, I thought to myself. *I'd rather be stung by bees!*

"How's it coming?" I asked him, taking a seat beside him on the porch.

"Many talismans. Many poems. Many more to do," he replied.

"I wish I could help, but I simply don't have your talent," I said.

"All art comes from the same source," Chief Leopard Frog observed.

"I reckon," I replied. "But I couldn't write a poem if my future depended on it."

"You photograph poems," Chief Leopard Frog said. "Very fine, very beautiful, revealing a magic world."

"Why, thank you, Chief. That's kind of you to say," I answered, sincerely flattered. "I'd like to be able to do more, but it's expensive."

"All art is costly to the artist," he replied. "Consider poetry. Each word must be torn from the heart. Very expensive. Very painful."

"Hmm," I said. "I hadn't thought of it like that."

I put a roll of film in my camera to photograph Chief Leopard Frog's work in progress. I figured that if nothing else, Milton Swartzman could use a snapshot for his catalog. Also, I wanted to record Chief Leopard Frog's art before it was dispersed throughout an unwary world. The detail in his carving, as always, was astonishing.

By the time the film came back from Sparkle Snapshot in St. Louis, Chief Leopard Frog had completed forty individual pieces and an equal number of new poems, each poem associated in some way with one of the carvings.

My feelings of guilt rose steadily, like the DRINK COCA-COLA IN BOTTLES thermometer outside Mel's (closed forever) Bait Shop on a summer day in Paisley, Kansas. Not just for hoodwinking Chief Leopard Frog, but also for unleashing Paisley's bad luck on an unprepared planet.

The talisman pictures turned out nicely. I also appreciated the bonus shot of Maureen Balderson in the bathtub. By now I'd come to expect such things, but this one was especially interesting. I'd forgotten what a nice smile she had.

"So," I said to Chief Leopard Frog, still staring at the picture of Maureen as he continued to carve bee tree burls, "what are you planning to call your book of poems?"

"Burl Hives," he replied.

"What?" I said. "That won't work. It sounds like some old country singer."

"It's my book," Chief Leopard Frog replied. "I can call it whatever I want."

"Yeah," I said, "but think about the marketing problem. Who's going to want to put out good money for a book of poems that sounds like it's about the guy who was Frosty the Snowman?"

"I did not ask you to write my book," Chief Leopard Frog said flatly. "Nor am I asking you to title my book. Only to send it to the man who will publish it. That is your role. Now excuse me while I carve."

What a nitwit, I thought. *That's the worst title imaginable.*

My feelings of guilt lessened somewhat.

I sneaked another peek at my most recent photo of Maureen Balderson before putting it away in the cigar box.

Too bad they moved away, I thought. *If it weren't for his Neanderthal killer instincts, her brother and I might have been friends.*

I sent a letter to Milton Swartzman, a brief situation report.

Dear Mr. Swartzman, I wrote.

We're about two-thirds of the way through the assignment. Making good progress, I think. There's just one hitch. My partner is expecting to get his poems published in a book. Somehow he got it into his head that you're the one who's going to publish it. Any ideas?

Sincerely,

Spencer Adams Honesty

P.S. That ghost camera is worth more than five hundred dollars. Take my word for it.

Careless Packing

I SPENT THE WEEKEND cutting back the pumpkin patch. It had grown so big that it was in danger of engulfing our home. Just up the road at Ma Puttering's place that very thing had already happened. Her house had vanished. There was nothing left but a house-shaped jungle of pumpkin vines.

"Where am I supposed to put all this stuff?" I asked my mother while chopping leaves as big as elephants' ears.

"Just pile it up by the road, and after it dries out, we'll burn it," she said.

"That'll be something to see," I commented.

Country people enjoy burning things. The entertainment value of the act far outweighs the damage to the atmosphere.

As Chief Leopard Frog was nearing the completion of his assignment, I turned my thoughts to practical matters:

How would I package and send the talismans? How would I deal with the "poetry issue"? How would I deposit the money, since no doubt it would come in the form of a check and there were no banks left in Paisley?

Plan ahead—that's my motto.

No, wait: that isn't true. *What's the rush?* is my motto.

Well, maybe they could both be my motto: *Plan ahead, but what's the rush?*

Seems okay.

Uncle Milton wrote back using regular mail. The stamp had a picture of the queen of England on it when she was much younger than she is today.

Dear Kid, he wrote.

At your suggestion, I have repriced the ghost camera at nine hundred ninety-nine dollars and ninety-five cents. I'll still give you ten percent off if you want it. The poetry book is a problem. I could print it for you when I print my catalog and it would be every bit as beautiful, but it would cost you. My guess is about three hundred dollars, but I'd have to check with my printing manager, and at the moment he's fishing. In the meantime, send me all the bad luck talismans you've got. An undeserving world awaits its comeuppance.

Your obedient servant,

Milton Swartzman

President and Publisher, Uncle Milton's Thousand Things You Thought You'd Never Find

P.S. The sample photo is excellent. Keep up the good work!

P.P.S. If you come across any unusual vegetables, such as pumpkins or gourds shaped like famous people, please let me know. I'm always on the lookout for a rare celebrity squash.

Dang! I thought to myself. *Just yesterday I threw away a baby gourd that resembled the former secretary of state Condoleezza Rice.*

I need to pay more attention.

That's what my motto should be: *Pay attention.*

Also, *What's the rush?* And *Plan ahead,* and *Take it easy.*

All of those.

I need a motto notebook, I thought.

It's lucky my mother was trained in post office procedures, because I would not have known how to ship a boxful of objects resembling five dozen withered apples all the way to the middle of the Caribbean Sea. I did know one thing, however. If they represented as much bad luck as Milton Swartzman believed they did, they'd better be packed carefully.

First, I wrapped each talisman in a page ripped from a catalog. Then I placed each one into a shipping box, gently, as if it were a mockingbird's egg, after which I filled the box with torn notebook paper. Then I placed the shipping box into an even larger shipping box, cushioned it all around with more paper, and sealed the whole thing airtight with nylon-reinforced packing tape.

You could drop this parcel from the moon and it would survive the fall, I figured. Besides, its contents were harder than walnuts.

The fastest way to get it there would have cost a fortune, so we settled on the patient way, estimated to take three weeks or more. In the meantime, there was nothing to do but . . .

See? That's the problem with living in Paisley.

There's nothing to do.

The mind is its own place, and itself
Can make a heav'n of hell, a hell of heav'n.
—Milton (the Italian poet of long ago,
no relation to Milton Swartzman)

"Any word yet?" Chief Leopard Frog asked the next day.

"Certainly not," I replied. "I doubt if the box has even left Kansas."

"Well, let me know the second you hear anything," Chief Leopard Frog requested.

"Yes, of course," I replied.

"I suppose I seem a little anxious," Chief Leopard Frog said.

"More than usual," I admitted.

"It's not the amulets I'm concerned about. They're easy to duplicate. It's the poems. They were my only copies," he explained.

"Which copies?" I asked.

"The ones I gave you," he replied.

"You gave me copies of your poems?" I said.

"You know I did," Chief Leopard Frog insisted. "I handed you a sheaf of papers while you were packing the box. Remember? You said, 'Thanks,' and I said, 'Don't mention it.' Remember?"

"Oh," I said, suddenly realizing what I had inadvertently done but not wishing to reveal my blunder to Chief Leopard Frog. "*Those* poems. Sure, I put them in the box with the talismans. Don't worry about a thing. They're winging their way to the Caribbean as we speak."

"Let me know when you hear something," he repeated.

"You bet," I told him. "You can count on me."

Not.

A Book Deal

I ALREADY FELT GUILTY about lying to my imaginary friend about the chances of his poems ever getting published. Now, when I thought about it, I had no reason left to live. I was a total wash-out. A liar, a loser, and a clumsy, absent-minded, self-absorbed oaf. I'd really blown it this time. I'd ripped all of Chief Leopard Frog's carefully crafted poems into packing material.

Yi, yi, yi, yi, yi! I thought. *Bring on the spiders! Bring on the bees! Let me take my own portrait with a ghost camera!*

I deserved to be the last kid in Paisley, Kansas.

Who could possibly want me for a friend?

After a sleepless night in my nest, I got up the next morning and sent a letter to Milton Swartzman.

Dear Mr. Swartzman:

Sixty "lucky" authentic Indian-carved bee tree burls are en route to you by Sushi Shipping Services. I expect you will receive them within your lifetime.

You will note that each is carefully packed in layers of paper to protect it from damage from rough seas and careless dockworkers. As it turns out, wadded up within this protective paper are the very poems that my friend wants published in a volume to be titled Burl Hives: Poems by Chief Leopard Frog, Sac and Fox Tribe, Paisley, Kansas.

Please don't ask me how the mix-up happened, as I feel bad enough as it is. Also don't give me any advice about the title because the author is adamant about his goofball choice.

You will recall that you said it would cost about three hundred dollars to print my friend's book. How many copies? And how will you handle distribution and national television appearances? Do you know Oprah? My mother watches her show all the time.

I am prepared to give up my three-hundred-dollar compensation for the talismans if we can work out a book deal. Please note, however, that I still need the money. As you suggested, I'm keeping an eye out for a famous-looking pumpkin. So far, I've got one that seems to be shaping up to look like the Wal-Mart smiley face. What would that be worth to you?

Sincerely,

Spencer Adams Honesty

Paisley, Kansas

A fortnight passed.

By now, September had just about sung its song.

Uncle Milton replied.

Dear Kid:

If all I do is exchange letters with you, how do you expect me to get any work done? No sign of your talismans yet, but I know the shipping line and they're as reliable as they come in this part of the world. I could do the book for the price we've agreed and print five hundred copies, which is all that the poetry world can possibly swallow, even if we were talking about the poet laureate of the Cayman Islands. I will send a dozen of them out for review to the leading journals and newspapers, hold back fifty copies for my catalog—it's definitely something you thought you'd never find—and send the remainder to you and your friend to peddle from the trunk of your car, which is basically the way poetry is meant to be distributed.

*If you ask me, which you didn't, you are wasting your money. I do
hope that you're doing this for the right reasons.*

Your obedient servant,

Milton Swartzman

President and Publisher, Uncle Milton's Thousand Things You
Thought You'd Never Find

*P.S. Don't try to con a con man, kid. Every pumpkin looks like the
Wal-Mart smiley face.*

*P.P.S. On the other hand, if you've got one that looks like Sam Wal-
ton, or even his wife, Helen, I could give you fifty bucks. His dog Ole
Roy is worth seventy-five.*

"Anything yet?" Chief Leopard Frog inquired, sticking his head
into my room.

"They're on the case," I assured him. "They're going to publish
it, but it'll take a while."

"Keep me informed," he insisted.

"Oh, I will," I said. "This means as much to me as it does
to you."

"Really?" he said. "How kind."

I was down to my last roll of film. After my morning shower,
I took a walk with my camera up toward Shiba Inu Ranch, where
once a Japanese American family raised prizewinning wide-eyed
dogs.

The roof to the house had caved in. The kennels had been removed and sold for scrap. Vegetation and fat grasshoppers ruled
the roost, so to speak.

I got a shot of one grasshopper head-on, staring into the lens.
I took one regular shot of the house, thinking that's the way to get
the ghost picture, and then I photographed a tiny white flower. A
bindweed, I think it's called.

From Shiba Inu Ranch I walked up to the Foo Farm, once a

thriving goat-raising enterprise, and according to local legend, run by a Wiccan, a member of a devil-worship cult. I found some bones there that were interesting to photograph—they looked like goat bones to me—plus I took pictures of the house and silo, which seemed to be in pretty good shape, all things considered.

On the way home, I took a few more shots at the Baldersons'. White mums were blooming by the porch, and the dust-covered window to Maureen's room looked interesting. I also found a keyless key chain in the dirt. It was gold-colored and bore the initial *M*.

Before pocketing the treasure, I photographed it.

Then, for some reason, my eyes filled with tears.

A Pumpkin Like Oprah

RETURNING FROM my latest photographic expedition, I found Chief Leopard Frog on the porch, whittling as always.

"Any news?" he asked.

"Not today," I replied. "Ask me again tomorrow."

Perhaps it is true that no matter where you live you spend much of your day doing things to avoid feeling lonely. Waiting for the mail, or waiting for a sandwich, is not exactly what you'd call a full, rich life. I was restless. I was bored. I was lonely.

I found myself thinking more and more about Maureen Balderson.

It occurred to me that I should write her a letter. Fortunately her forwarding address was filed in my mother's office, along with the forwarding addresses of everybody else who'd lived in Paisley and knew where they were headed.

Less than half, by the way.

Dear Maureen: I wrote, then scratched out the word *Dear,* then wadded up the paper and started over.

Maureen:

Do you miss Paisley? It's still a nice place even though everybody's gone. I've been taking pictures of it before it is reduced to rubble,

vegetation, and predatory insects, the portraits of some of which I en-
close with this letter. I have had a couple of unfortunate run-ins with
bees, broke my collarbone, and sustained a few other injuries climbing
Heath's, and have recently begun working in the publishing business.

Hope you're fine.

Please write back when you have time.

Sincerely,

Spencer Adams Honesty

P.S. Tell your brother hi for me.

P.P.S. Your mailbox still stands. I enclose a photo.

After that, I got lonelier and lonelier. Sometimes I just sat outside for hours on the swing suspended from the walnut tree, doing
nothing but watching chipmunks and birds. Interestingly, this
passivity paid off, for it wasn't long before they let me take their
pictures without scurrying away.

One day, a red fox family wandered through the yard, a mother
and four kits. They looked at me as if I were a rock or a tree and
kept going.

Chief Leopard Frog asked about the mail every single day.

He had become a real pain in the butt.

"These things take time," I reminded him.

"It's my first book," he reminded me. "Understandably, I'm
anxious."

I got a postcard from Maureen. It showed a picture of a herd of
buffalo. On the back of it she wrote:

Dear Twerp: Thanks for the swell bug pix. Dang, they're ugly!
Kansas City is a big place. It has more than two hundred McDonald's
restaurants. Can you imagine? As long as you're taking pictures, will
you break in to my house and take some pictures of my room? I miss
it. I even miss you from time to time, but not that much. Sincerely,
your pal, MO.

P.S. My brother is a nuisance. I'm not telling him anything.

I can't tell you how much this postcard cheered me.

I felt as if I'd won a prize or something. I felt excited, liberated, connected to a real world, in touch with a person who knew me and understood me, an individual whom, as fate would have it, I found attractive. I carried that buffalo photo with me for days until it became sweat stained and the message on the back turned blurry.

Reluctantly, lest it disintegrate entirely, I put it into the cigar box with my other prized possessions, including Maureen's key chain.

Here's a special message for everybody who's thinking about killing himself: What's the rush? Not only will things change, but they often change suddenly. This is true even when you live in an unlucky town.

The next morning when I went out to the pumpkin patch I found waiting for me a fully formed pumpkin that was a dead ringer for Oprah Winfrey.

I called my mother immediately.

"Look at this," I commanded excitedly. "Who does it look like?"

"My God," she said. "It's Oprah."

Immediately, we packed it up and shipped it to Milton Swartzman the fast way.

I enclosed a note.

There's lots more where this came from, I claimed optimistically. *Please pay shipping and the fifty bucks you promised and I'll keep 'em coming.*

The following week the FedEx man (whose name turned out to be Dwight Earl) stopped at the house with a letter and inquired about the possibility of a meal.

My mother turned off the television, ran into the bathroom to brush her hair, then raced downstairs to the kitchen to begin melting Crisco.

Heck, it wasn't just *my* luck that was changing. It was everybody's—even Dwight Earl's.

The Magic Touch

THE OPRAH LOOK-ALIKE pumpkin had done the trick!

Inside the FedEx letter pack was a check from *Uncle Milton's Thousand Things You Thought You'd Never Find* for eighty-nine dollars and fifty-five cents, representing the cost of shipping the pumpkin plus fifty dollars.

Dear Kid, Milton wrote.

Now we're talking! Your Oprah pumpkin is already in the Ripley's Believe It or Not Museum in Branson, Missouri, where it is drawing very large crowds, I hear. Good job. The talismans are selling well, mostly to a regional voodoo group, but business is business. The poetry book (what a mess!) will be out soon. I may only keep five copies for the catalog, now that I've read it. You can have the rest. Tell your Indian friend to take his time writing a sequel.

Yours truly,

Milton Swartzman

President and Publisher, Uncle Milton's Thousand Things You Thought You'd Never Find

P.S. I sold the camera to a guy in Egypt who plans to use it to photograph pharaohs who may still be drifting around ancient tombs. Whatever! To repeat myself, business is business.

P.P.S. Thanks for sharing the monster insect photos. Have you ever considered putting them all together into a book? I like the title "As Cute as a Bug's Ear." It's an old-fashioned expression, but the grannies will go nuts for it.

Dwight Earl really enjoyed the fried chicken dinner. My mother even made him a blueberry pie. After dinner he took her for a ride in his truck. Then she took him for a ride in her truck. I found it interesting that they had so much in common.

While my mind was on other things the landscape of Paisley once again was changing. Overnight, it seemed, the abandoned pastures were filled with bright yellow sunflowers, a gnarly, weedy creation that for a few weeks when fall approaches bursts into a sunshine yellow sea. Along the fallen fencerows, trumpet vines bloomed, mauve, pink, brick red, and violet fairy hats surrounding the sunflower celebration. Mailbox posts and utility poles hoisted blue-eyed morning glories up into the sky, where some bloomed triumphantly all day long.

Together they turned Paisley into baroque music, into a French impressionist painting, into a sight to take your breath away, all without the assistance of a single Paisley resident, except myself, to pause and take it all in.

I shot lots of pictures of this piece and that piece, but with my camera it is impossible to capture the vastness, the riot of color, the majestic glory of all of Paisley, Kansas, in the cusp of fall.

With a fresh source of funds, I could afford more film and processing. After returning from a trip to Wal-Mart with my mother and Dwight Earl, I sauntered over to the Balderson house next door.

There was a FOR SALE sign out front, but, like the flowers in the fields, no one had seen it but me. Already it had begun to rust and was tilted precariously like the Leaning Tower of Pisa. Three white mushrooms—the deadly poisonous *Amanita muscaria*—sprouted at its post, as if some unseen force was warning would-be buyers away.

For Maureen's amusement, I took a picture.

Her house was locked, as I expected it to be. I knew better than to break anything. For one, it's not neighborly. For another, broken locks and windows are not easily fixable when there are no handymen left in town.

Her room was on the second floor at the back. I'd already had some experience as a second-story man, and it had been a disappointing experience, at best.

I walked around to the back to evaluate the situation, which is where I found Chief Leopard Frog whittling yet another bee tree burl amulet.

"Hey," I said.

"What's up?" he replied.

"I was trying to figure out how to get upstairs to take some pictures," I told him.

No sense lying any more to Chief Leopard Frog.

"Why not take the stairs?" he asked.

"The place is locked up tight," I replied.

"Not if you hurry," Chief Leopard Frog said.

At my touch, the back door swung open.

A Quirky Debut

ONCE INSIDE THE BALDERSON HOUSE, I ran up the stairs to Maureen's room. I knew it was hers because it had posters on the wall of boy bands that nobody but Maureen had ever heard of: The Riffs. The Ruffs. The Riff-Raffs. The Rough Roofs. The Rafters. The Raptors.

You get the idea.

There was also a stuffed bear in a corner, a little multicolored threadbare bear, as if inadvertently left behind in the rush to leave, but nevertheless an artifact with the appearance of personal importance.

I set my camera carefully. I took pictures of everything that seemed to matter, including a butterfly sticker on a wall switch, a telephone number scrawled in ballpoint pen on a white windowsill, a carpet stain created by spilled nail polish, a hair clip in a dusty corner.

On my way out I nabbed the bear and took a picture of the door, closed, as a way of saying goodbye.

Back downstairs, I found Chief Leopard Frog continuing to whittle.

"All done?" he asked.

"I guess so," I answered.

"She's older than you," he observed.

"I'm just trying to be friends," I said.

"She lives very far away," he added. "Three days' walk for an Indian. Many more for you."

"I'm just doing a favor for a friend," I explained.

"Here," Chief Leopard Frog said. "Take this. It may come in handy."

He handed me the talisman he had just completed. It was in the shape of a tiny alligator. I was somewhat reluctant to accept it, knowing what Uncle Milton had reported about Chief Leopard Frog's "good luck" pieces, but I pocketed it nevertheless, believing that in the same way rock breaks scissors, scissors cut paper, and paper covers rock, friendship overwhelms bad luck.

A fortnight later I received a package from Sparkle Snapshot of St. Louis containing prints and negatives from several rolls of film.

There were many lovely compositions featuring flowers and mushrooms and mailboxes; a rather formal portrait of the Shiba Inu family standing on their front porch without a single smile among them; a couple of action shots of the Foos engaged in repairing a vacuum cleaner; and a full roll of exposures of Maureen.

That's when I knew for a fact how terribly lonely I was.

That night, as I sifted through the twenty-four photos of my former next-door neighbor, I cried myself to sleep, and not just manly sniff-sniff all-choked-up crying, either, or stiff-upper-lip eyes welling up with tears, but real, all-out, pillow-watering, chest-heaving blubbering.

I had been overwhelmed by photographs of Maureen talking on the phone, Maureen stretching her foot to the end of the bed, Maureen picking up something to put into the wastebasket, Maureen drying her hair, Maureen brushing her teeth, Maureen changing a CD, Maureen exercising on the floor, Maureen eating a cup of Jell-O, Maureen putting on a nightgown, Maureen practicing ballet, Maureen staring out the window, Maureen, her head on her pillow, fast asleep.

Damn you, ghost camera! I thought. *If it weren't for you I might have forgotten her by now.*

The next day Dwight Earl brought a box from the Cayman Islands. He stayed for supper. Catfish and hush puppies. While the thick chunks of breaded catfish sizzled in the pan, my mother quickly changed into her Sunday best.

The box was quite heavy. With Dwight Earl's help I carried it upstairs to my room.

"What's in it?" he asked.

"Aren't you guys supposed to keep mum about the contents of what you deliver to people?" I asked. "Like the relationship between a lawyer and his client, or a priest and a petitioner?"

"Nobody ever told me that," Dwight Earl said. "I like to know what's inside. It's like Christmas. Heck, if I weren't worried about getting fired, I'd open 'em all."

"That's the trouble with this country," I observed, cutting the tape along the top with a blunt pair of scissors. "Nobody can keep a secret."

Dwight Earl peered over my shoulder.

"Well, you'd better go find Chief Leopard Frog," I announced, "because it looks like his opus has arrived."

"Who?" Dwight Earl asked.

"Never mind," I said. "It's just a box of books."

"Too bad," Dwight Earl replied, leaving the room. "I was hoping for something edible."

Chief Leopard Frog was furious with me.

"How could you let this happen?" he hollered.

If he'd had a tomahawk on him, I suspect he might have used it on me.

"This is a travesty!" he continued. "It's worse than not publishing them at all."

"Oh, I don't know," I said, leafing through the flimsy newsprint pages. "It's sort of interesting—in a quirky way."

"Who needs quirky?" he demanded. "Certainly not a first-time author! My career is over before it's begun, and it's all your fault!"

The words echoed in my head:

"It's all your fault!"

Poetry Means Never Having
to Say You're Sorry

CHIEF LEOPARD FROG had a right to be upset, all things considered.

In his effort to restore the poems to their original, pristine, pre-torn condition, Uncle Milton apparently also recovered a handful of catalog pages that got mixed in with the poems much as if you'd put all the words together into a poppy red KitchenAid twelve-speed blender.

For example, one of Chief Leopard Frog's thoughtful observations on the south wind pushing incessantly across the dry Kansas plain was merged with text from a Japanese soap manufacturer to create such phrases as "The softly swirling dry heat on which crisp grasshoppers take flight closes pores and raises mountainous thunderheads to burnish the flat landscape into a more resilient, more radiant, younger-looking you."

Another one somehow mixed the smoothness of a flat rock at the bottom of a Colorado stream with the outstanding fuel efficiency of the new Toyota Highlander.

My favorite, called "Death of a Harmless Varmint," described the unfortunate demise of a young prairie dog at the hands of the government in the context of a Cuban seed cigar wrapped in a green candela wrapper "just like the young shock-haired president enjoyed after the Cuban embargo."

But the real clincher was the page from the sex toy catalog that got merged with Chief Leopard Frog's sentimental remembrance of his late mother. This one he could not possibly forgive me for, not that I could blame him.

Indeed, the least offensive phrase, "Tickle her fancy until her fancy can't stand it anymore," was juxtaposed with a detailed description of the dry earth "hitting her coffin one shovelful at a time to make a sound like lamentations emitted by a buckskin drum."

Well, at least they'd gotten the title right. BURL HIVES, it said in big block letters on the cover. POEMS BY CHIEF LEOPARD FROG, SAC AND FOX TRIBE, PAISLEY, KANSAS.

But then Uncle Milton Swartzman, ever the salesman, had gone on to phony up a cover quote:

> *The world of poetry will never be the same*
> *now that one daring Native American*
> *has so boldly wrested control from*
> *the insensitive white man.*
> —Carl Sandburg

Never mind that Carl Sandburg had been dead for years.

Chief Leopard Frog was not amused by Uncle Milton casting his work as an ongoing struggle with whites for Native American recognition.

And to think, I thought, *this nightmare cost me three hundred dollars!*

Here's an example of what I was going to have to deal with:

THE RAVEN CALLS
By Chief Leopard Frog

Pin feather, tail feather, wing feather, beak
The Tempur-Pedic Swedish Sleep System can't be beat
Down he hurls from pinnacle and peak
The Euro-Bed by Tempur-Pedic guarantees sleep
He calls the wild wind as he calls the slumbering me
The pressure-relieving comfort is extraordinary
Nevermore?
I disagree.
Forevermore is far more likely.
It's the latest in NASA-endorsed technology
Bird becoming human becoming spirit becoming god
Microfiber suede textile sample, free video
Indian blood.

Within a fortnight the post office at Paisley was overwhelmed. My mother, increasingly annoyed, missed *Oprah* three days in a row because of the need to sort mail for Chief Leopard Frog.

"Who is this guy, anyway?" she complained. "I thought I knew everybody within fifty miles of here."

"He's a transient," I explained. "Basically, a time transient. But I can get his stuff to him. Just give it to me."

"Dang," she muttered. "If I had known that raising kids would be like this. Time transients. Indian chiefs. Two hundred pounds of first-class mail. Lord love a duck! Where will it ever end?"

Of course, as should have been expected, *The New Yorker* declared Chief Leopard Frog's debut tome to be "brilliant beyond belief."

The *New York Review of Books* claimed in a five-thousand-word essay, "Here, at last, is the long-awaited amalgamation of the first America with the second. In a literary sense, *Burl Hives* is the authentic missing link."

Praise was pouring in from everywhere. Invitations to appear on television, at dinner, at receptions to receive awards and honorary degrees. Offers from other publishers throwing out astounding numbers. A letter from the wife of the former president of the United States.

What you've captured in a few simple words is so us, she wrote. *I hope you are not offended when I say you are the Norman Rockwell of our age.*

Cordially,

(Mrs.) Laura Bush

P.S. What is your e-mail address?

And orders.

Hundreds and hundreds of orders for the book from all over the world.

As a poet, Chief Leopard Frog was off to the races!

The Accidental Poet

MIXED IN WITH the worldwide acclaim for the work of Chief Leopard Frog was a desperate plea from the Cayman Islands.

Dear Partner, Milton Swartzman wrote

(*Partner?* I thought. *Since when have Uncle Milton and I become partners?*)

Help. Send me more copies of the Indian's poetry book until I can print some more down here. The demand is unlike anything I've ever seen, including the scratch 'n' sniff fake vomit that put my kids through college. This Indian friend of yours must know what he's doing.

Yours affectionately,

Milton Swartzman

President and Publisher, Uncle Milton's Thousand Things You Thought You'd Never Find

P.S. That gourd that looked like Lindsay Lohan was okay, but I had no takers until I dressed it in a swimsuit. Didn't I always say it was about salesmanship? I enclose fifty dollars—no, make it sixty dollars. Hope it comes in handy.

If nothing else, the sixty dollars came in handy for buying stamps and small manila envelopes for sending books to people who ordered them by check. Uncle Milton had put a fifteen-dollar price on the book, and while that seemed high to me, it didn't seem to dissuade the American public.

My mother and I had to change our routine. We went to the city twice a week now just to deposit checks. My hand grew tired from all the endorsing I had to do.

Yet it was not my name that I was writing. Each time I signed a check, I had to sign the name of Chief Leopard Frog. That I knew he was imaginary was something I figured I'd best keep to myself. No point in spilling the beans to the whole world just yet. And certainly not to the bank.

Interestingly, the chief hadn't shown his face since the day he'd lost his temper. I knew he was furious, but come on, shouldn't his curiosity have prompted him to look in on things? How long are you supposed to stay mad at somebody before it becomes an affliction?

Some of the mail was not so nice. One letter from the lawyer representing the estate of the late singer Burl Ives threatened to sue. Another, from the director of the Carl Sandburg Foundation and Museum, said he'd been in touch with the Burl Ives lawyer and was thinking of suing also—sort of a tag team. A couple of Indian tribes from Minnesota and Wyoming accused me of making the whole thing up, claiming there were no chiefs of the Sac and Fox tribe left in Kansas, but they enclosed complimentary coupons for free nights at their casino hotels, nevertheless.

I got some snapshots back from Sparkle Snapshot in St. Louis, and one of them was a real good picture of my missing toe—like a medical study. There was also a picture of Chief Leopard Frog on the front porch, hunched over and whittling an alligator talisman. His hair was pulled back into a ponytail and his nose seemed sort of like that of a gargoyle on the side of a tall granite building. Even so, he was an imposing presence, as much as someone can be in an amateur photo. I should add that it was the only picture of Chief Leopard Frog I'd ever seen.

There was also a snapshot of Maureen, her fingertips together as if in contemplation. The lighting was such that the dimple in her right cheek was quite pronounced.

Then a reporter showed up from *Poetry Week* magazine.

That's when the trouble started.

The opposite of boredom is excitement. And the definition of excitement is "a sustained period of anxiety."

Be careful what you wish for. Be especially careful when you choose to rearrange a quiet, peaceful life. The day may come when you will miss watching pumpkins grow.

Merilee Rowling was a stringer for a big, wealthy poetry magazine back east. It used to be a little, insignificant poetry magazine back east, but then a famous, rich, and somewhat empty-headed widow of a hamburger czar died and left the magazine her vast fortune. Now the magazine felt inclined not just to publish poetry but to investigate poetry and poets.

Holy smokes!

Investigative poetry.

How did they come up with *that* idea?

Now the reporter was on my doorstep.

"I've looked everywhere for somebody breathing in this godforsaken town," she said. "You're my last hope. Do you actually live here?"

"Have you checked the motel?" I asked.

"What motel?" she replied.

"Then I guess you have," I replied. "Welcome to Paisley."

"Actually," she explained, her car still running in the front yard, "I'm looking for some Indian chief—Bullfrog, Tree Frog, Hopping Frog, something like that."

"The only Indian chief around here is named Chief Leopard Frog," I said.

"That's the one!" she exclaimed. "I need to talk to him right away."

"What's the rush?" I asked. "If you want to see the chief, you'll have to learn to be patient."

Patience, apparently, was not one of Miss Merilee Rowling's virtues.

A Gland Night Out

THE HEADSTRONG YOUNG STRANGER stood defiantly at my doorstep, demanding an audience with Chief Leopard Frog.

"And whom shall I say is calling?" I replied as formally as I could under the circumstances.

"The assistant to the assistant editor for light features for *Poetry Week* magazine," she announced with considerable pride. "Miss Merilee Rowling."

"Have you had lunch?" I asked.

"They serve lunch around here?" she replied. "Where?"

"I can make you a tomato sandwich," I told her. "Do you like mayonnaise?"

"I'd eat anything," she said. "It took me forever to find this place, and I'm famished."

"Please come in," I said, although as events would turn out, I should have said, "Please go back the way you came."

Since mail was stacked up on all the kitchen countertops, we had our sandwiches in the living room. Merilee Rowling sat in my dead grandmother's rocking chair. I sat on the torn sofa.

"What happened to this town?" Merilee Rowling asked between bites.

"Bad luck," I answered. "Same as lots of towns."

"I live in a big city," she said. "Our bad luck comes and goes and nobody notices."

"Everybody noticed here," I explained. "That's why they left."

"Hmm," said Merilee Rowling. "Yet one of the country's greatest undiscovered poets stayed."

"I guess you could say that," I replied. "Would you care for some chips?"

"Sure, anything," she answered. "Chips, Fritos, pork rinds—whatever you've got."

To my mind, Merilee Rowling didn't look any older than Maureen Balderson, but I suppose she had to be, because she had a job and had driven a car all the way from back east, and you don't do that if you're fifteen years old.

It turned out that Merilee Rowling was seventeen, almost eighteen, and had just gotten out of high school. She decided not to go to college because, as she put it, "How can you see the world if you're stuck in one place?"

I thought about that one long and hard.

"So you've seen the world?" I asked.

"Not all of it," she replied. "But I've seen a lot more than I'd seen by this time last year."

"And how does Paisley stack up?" I inquired.

Merilee Rowling choked on a Triscuit.

"You must be kidding," she said.

As our conversation continued, a blaze burst up beside the road in front of the house. My mother was burning dried pumpkin leaves.

"Maybe you should turn your car off," I suggested. "Just for safety's sake. Plus, if you run out of gas, you won't see any more of the world except Paisley."

"Oh my gosh!" she exclaimed. "How careless of me."

When she jumped up from the rocking chair I noticed for the first time how cute she was. She reminded me of a girl I'd seen on TV, a guest on *Oprah,* who was starring in a new TV series, something about witches and high school.

Why does it take me so long to notice things? Is it because I'm not looking through my camera?

While Merilee Rowling was outside dealing with her car and, unfortunately, meeting my pyromaniac mother, I recalled a story I'd read when I was merely a child, no more than six years old.

It was about two children, a boy and a girl, who'd been skating on a frozen pond, something commonplace in the olden days, and although they knew each other, they were merely neighbors, outside to enjoy whatever frolic winter affords.

Alas, as fate would have it, they fell through a patch of thin ice—certain death under most circumstances—but a kindly old woman saved them, got them out of their wet clothes, and tucked them into a feather bed, where she covered them with thick down comforters and brought them steaming pots of chamomile tea while drying their clothes on a rack by the fire.

In a way, the story was the opposite of the fairy tales in which the witch entices children into her sugarplum house only to toss them into the oven for dinner. I suppose that's why whoever wrote the story decided to write it. A good deed–doer protective of the happy ending.

But what I recalled from the story was something other than the kindness of a stranger.

I remembered the thrilling thought of being naked under the covers with a girl whom I knew but didn't know that well. I remembered it as being an exciting, exhilarating idea, a stroke of good fortune, and a reasonable outcome to pursue for one's entire life.

Some people think that children don't have such thoughts, but these people have forgotten what it is like to be a child.

As I say, I couldn't have been much older than six. Now, in my early adolescence, the idea seemed even more compelling.

What if, I thought, *I could persuade Merilee Rowling to stay overnight at my house?*

This was Paisley, Kansas. It was getting late. Where else could she go?

It's not as if Maureen Balderson would ever need to know, I assured myself.

Heh, heh, heh, I chuckled to myself, proud of the grandiosity of my sudden cleverness. *Perhaps homeschooling isn't such a bad idea after all.*

The Night Visitor

WHERE *WAS* HE?

Chief Leopard Frog, who should have been around to offer consultation on a subject as big as this one, namely, the entrapment of a stranger, was nowhere to be found.

What a petulant, petty man he was turning out to be!

The screen door swung open and clouds of smoke followed Merilee Rowling and my mother inside.

"Spencer," my mother said, "did you know that this poor girl has traveled all the way from back east and has nowhere to stay the night?"

"That's terrible," I said insincerely.

Then I applied a little bit of psychology.

"Maybe she could stay at the Baldersons'," I suggested. "If we could figure out how to get the place unlocked."

"Nonsense," my mother replied. "She'll do no such thing. She can stay right here in this house with us. Our home may be modest, but as long as the Lord gives us breath in our bodies, we'll always have room for one more."

"Actually," I said, to no one's understanding or approval, "if one of us were suddenly to stop breathing, there'd be room for an additional person, wouldn't there? So the Lord providing us with breath in our bodies is really something of an impediment, accommodation-wise."

"Spencer," my mother instructed, "you may sleep on the couch. Merilee Rowling will take your room."

"Now everybody just hold on a minute," I objected. "I have personal items in my room. I don't want some stranger poking around in there."

Merilee Rowling glared at me. She had high cheekbones and wide eyes like the girls on the covers of catalogs. I liked that.

"Oh, really, Spencer," Merilee Rowling said. "Do I look like a snoop?"

Now, what kind of question is that? This girl had just driven a thousand miles to get the skinny on a nonexistent Native American accidental poet, and she wanted to know if I thought she was capable of going through my stuff?

Holy macaroni! I thought. *She's not just a snoop. She's a professional snoop.*

It seemed that I'd already lost control of the situation. My timing was months off. Merilee Rowling should have waited until January to show up. Then we could have gone ice-skating on Craddock Pond before we chose rooms.

But who would have saved us when we broke through the ice? Paisley was deserted.

Hmm, I thought. *Even the simplest of fantasies can become too complicated.*

"Well, at least let me collect my valuables," I muttered, meaning my cigar box filled with photos, my ghost camera, my toothbrush, and a change of clothes.

"Spencer," my mother said, "how did you get to be so rude?"

"Is there anything I can do to help you prepare dinner, Mrs.

Honesty?" Merilee Rowling asked. "I'm quite good at slicing vegetables."

"Well, I guess I could use some help with the pumpkin pie," my mother replied. "Do you enjoy baking?"

"It's my favorite pastime," Merilee Rowling replied.

What? I thought. *First you give this girl my room, and now you're trusting her with knives? This is not turning out at all as I had hoped!*

A scream awoke the household in the middle of the night. It came from my room. I lay on the lumpy sofa and considered investigating. On the one hand, there was the siren call of my pillow. On the other, obvious trouble upstairs. Possibly serious. Possibly not.

What to do, what to do, I wondered in a half slumber.

"Spencer!" my mother shouted. "Get up here now!"

I found the two women in my room, my mother seated beside Merilee Rowling with her arm around her shoulders, comforting her. I noticed that Merilee Rowling was wearing one of my T-shirts.

"Spencer, Merilee says there was a man in her room," my mother announced.

"Was he wearing a FedEx uniform?" I asked.

My mother glared at me.

"He was wearing an Indian headdress," Merilee Rowling said with a sad little sniff.

"Oh, that would be Chief Leopard Frog," I explained. "Did you get your interview?"

"Are you crazy?" Merilee Rowling responded. "I was too scared to think. Anyway, the guy gave me the creeps."

"He has that effect on some people," I agreed. "Well, good night."

"Wait a minute, Spencer," my mother commanded. "Aren't you going to do something?"

"Huh?" I said. "Oh, yeah." I leaned over and kissed my mother on the cheek.

"Night, Mom," I said, turning to go back downstairs.

"No, Spencer," my mother said. "I mean, about the situation concerning our houseguest. She's traumatized."

"Oh, all right," I replied.

I leaned over and kissed Merilee Rowling on the cheek.

"You jerk!" Merilee Rowling responded, wiping her cheek with her hand. "I don't want your slobbery kisses. I want you to stay in this room with me for the rest of the night."

Was I hearing this correctly? Or was it the sound of ice cracking on distant Craddock Pond?

"I see no reason why you can't sleep on the floor, Spencer," my mother said, "to protect Merilee from any more intrusions by that spooky so-called friend of yours. You owe her that much."

"The couch is lumpy, but at least it's a soft lumpy," I complained. "The floor is nothing but boards. Why can't she just scoot over?"

"That, Spencer, as you well know, would be improper," my mother pronounced, "although I don't expect you at your age to understand why."

Ha! I thought. *Sez you!*

It Happened One Night

WELL, WHO WOULD'VE THUNK IT, I thought. *I've got seventeen-year-old Merilee Rowling in my room. No, not just in my room. In my* bed!

Spencer Adams Honesty.

The last kid in Paisley, Kansas.

I hauled up a few sofa cushions and quilts and fashioned on the floor the same sort of nest I was accustomed to sleeping in when the bed belonged to me. I couldn't see Merilee Rowling from where I was curled up, but I could certainly hear every sound she made, and it was pretty clear to me that she wasn't sleeping.

"What's on your mind?" I asked.

"You," she said.

"How's that?" I inquired.

"I was thinking I might be better off with the Indian," she explained. "You don't strike me as being old enough to have developed a code of honor."

"What do you mean, 'code of honor'?" I asked.

"In the days of old when knights and their royal ladies had to travel together and it came time to sleep, the knight would place his sword between them as a sign that he would not cross over while she slept. This was an important part of the knight's code of honor."

"No problemo," I replied. "I'll just fetch that pie knife from downstairs. Okay with you if there's still some pumpkin goo on it?"

"I'm not certain you understand," Merilee Rowling said. "How old are you, again?"

"Nineteen," I lied, adding some six years to my life in a single stroke. "But I'm small for my age. I had a rare disease when I was a child."

"Yeah, you had a disease, all right," Merilee Rowling retorted. "You had bullshit disease."

"We're hoping for a cure," I answered.

"There isn't one," Merilee Rowling replied. "Trust me. I know."

"You mean like your favorite activity being baking? Is that what you mean?" I asked knowingly.

Merilee Rowling giggled.

"Oh, all right, you caught me," she said. "But I was just trying to be a good houseguest."

"Well, in your own special way, you are, Merilee Rowling," I said. "Anyway, good night. And don't worry. I'll keep an eye out for Indians."

"Thank you, Spencer," she replied. "And I'm sorry for doubting your code of honor."

And that was it until the next morning and the half-hour wait for the bathroom.

I couldn't stand having Chief Leopard Frog angry with me. The chief and I go back a long way, back to a time when I really needed a father and instead, after a whole lot of wishing, I got Chief Leopard Frog, who in many ways was better than a father.

Sometimes I'd mention to my mother that he'd told me something and she'd just smile and say, "That's nice." But I don't think she ever believed in him. The thing is, with an imaginary friend, no matter what age you are you have to be willing to suspend your everyday disbeliefs.

I've known people who've seen angels, received secret messages from ghosts, and had long conversations with Jesus (who must be terribly busy). I've known people who jabbered with their dead ancestors or wives or husbands as if they were standing right beside them.

Who am I to say they're mistaken?

And who are they to say that Chief Leopard Frog is nothing but a figment of my imagination?

Mr. Riley, who once lived three miles down the road before he went to live with his daughter in Florida, used to talk to his dog Flag all the time, and Flag had been dead and buried for five years!

I used to leave pork bones on Flag's grave.

Mr. Riley wouldn't make a decision without first talking it over with Flag. Heck, it was Flag who'd said, "Let's go to Florida and see the sights."

There are millions of people who talk to their cats. How many cats are listening? There are people who talk to goldfish, and hamsters, and parakeets, and I've read in magazines about scientists—educated people—who talk to plants.

Potted plants.

When we pray, to whom do we pray?

When we ask for forgiveness, whom are we asking to forgive us? Ourselves?

I found Chief Leopard Frog squatting underneath a walnut tree, whittling a talisman in the shape of a pony.

"I wish you'd let me explain," I said.

"I know what happened," he replied. "I figured it out."

"It's turned out well," I went on. "Commercially speaking."

"That's good luck, then," he said.

"Yes," I agreed. "Very good luck."

"Bad art, though," Chief Leopard Frog added. "Aesthetically speaking."

"Who's to say what art is?" I asked. "The sender or the receiver?"

"You may have something there, Spencer," Chief Leopard Frog observed, thawing just a little bit. "Who's the girl?"

"Someone looking for you," I answered. "A poetry writer. She wants to make you famous, but you scared her last night."

"I was looking for you," he said.

"I figured," I replied. "What'd you want?"

"To say I'm sorry for my anger," he explained. "Not for my disappointment. I'm entitled to that. But it was wrong to blame you for events."

I held out my hand.

"Friends?" I said.

He covered it with his own while at the same time placing the freshly carved pony into my grasp.

"Always," Chief Leopard Frog said.

Thinking of You

IN OVER MY HEAD, I sought practical advice from a man in daily contact with ancient wisdom.

"What shall I do about this visitor?" I asked Chief Leopard Frog.

"Ha!" he laughed loudly. "An excellent question. Give me a few days to ponder the answer."

Back at the house, my mother and Merilee Rowling were laughing and carrying on like old friends while they sorted the mountain of mail, most of it for Chief Leopard Frog, but one letter for me was from Maureen Balderson, plus a packet from Sparkle Snapshot and a small box from the Cayman Islands.

There's an old saying—as least I'm told it's an old saying; I'm not exactly old enough to know how old the sayings are—but at any rate it goes, "Be careful what you wish for. You just might get it."

But have I mentioned that already?

Like many sayings, this one is a trifle vague, but I think it means that if you're wishing you had excitement in your life and all of a sudden you're dealing with the bruised egos of sensitive imaginary Indians, and the sudden bursting forth of motherly behavior by a former television vegetable, and the unannounced arrival of a smart-aleck cutie-pie way too old for you, and letters from modern-day pirates of the Caribbean, not to mention notes from girls who once lived next door and the occasional unexplained photograph of a vanished person, well, it's like that other old saying that goes, "It's either feast or famine."

Suddenly I had too much to do.

I could feel the pressure building.

I think I liked it better when I was bored.

The giggling subsided when I entered the room.

"You've got quite a few book orders here, Spencer, which I presume you will process promptly," my mother said, like she was giving instructions, "and there's some personal mail for you as well."

"Your son appears to be quite a popular person," Merilee Rowling observed. "It must be a trait he acquired from his mother."

"Aww," my mother said, brushing away the transparent compliment with her hand. "I've never seen him with anyone at all. Not even that Indian friend of his."

"Really?" Merilee Rowling responded, looking me square in the eye. "How interesting."

"I think I'll read my mail now," I announced.

For some reason I was afraid to open Maureen's note, so I opened the package from Uncle Milton Swartzman instead. Inside was a conch shell that had been polished and fitted with a mouthpiece and a muting device such as you'd find on a trumpet. There was also a check for five thousand and fifty dollars, plus two pieces of paper.

One a letter.

One a contract.

Dear Partner, Uncle Milton wrote.

Have you ever heard of an ocarina? It is an ancient flutelike device that in the right hands plays lovely, haunting sounds that remind some of us of the sea. Well, this is a concharina, a device of my own creation that is a steady seller in the catalog. I wanted you to have it as an expression of our friendship. Ditto the five grand. I have enclosed a one-page contract for you and your Indian pal to sign. Basically, it says I can keep printing the poetry book so long as I keep sending you twenty percent of the gross. In the publishing business, that's known as a sweet deal for the writer and his agent, because I take care of everything. You don't have to lift a finger, except to get your friend to write more books when he's ready. Who knew this would be such a hit? Already it has outsold the life-size talking reproduction of the Jackalope.

Earnestly yours,
Milton Swartzman
President and Publisher, Uncle Milton's Thousand Things You Thought You'd Never Find

P.S. Thanks for the gourd that looks exactly like the late Sammy Davis, Jr. I like it so much that I am keeping it for myself. The extra fifty is for your effort.

P.P.S. Don't forget to send along some more bad luck talismans whenever you can. I don't want to wear out Chief Golden Goose, but I'm developing a very specialized clientele for his whittling. Military types and self-appointed officials from countries you've never heard of. 'Nuff said.

The note from Maureen was written on a card, the kind you search for in the aisles of Hallmark Gold Crown stores for a long time until you happen upon just the right one. This one showed two people standing underneath a garden bower. They were kissing.

Inside, the printed part said, *Thinking of you.*

Maureen had added a handwritten note:

Guess what? she said. *We may be coming back for a few days to check on the house. I'll let you know.*

Hugs,
Mo

P.S. Thanks for the swell pix of me in my room. I don't know how you managed to do it, but it was fun to get them.

Again and again, I returned to the picture of the lovers on the cover of the card. It took a while before my breathing returned to normal.

Picture Day

When you get mail, mail call is truly an exciting part of the day.

Unexpected riches from Uncle Milton. A love note (of sorts) from Maureen Balderson. And still I hadn't opened the packet of prints from Sparkle Snapshot of St. Louis.

By now I'd totally lost track of what I had taken pictures of, but the giant clover flowers and yellow sprays of wildflowers that looked like baby's breath and one enormous mosquito on a screen door were quite good. The rapid-fire sequence of the wide-mouthed toad in the garden made me laugh out loud, but toads, of course, are naturally funny creatures.

As always, it was the bonus picture that gave me pause. Two children had fallen through the ice in a frozen pond.

One of them clearly was me. I recognized my stupid mole.

The other was Maureen.

Sigh.

"I notice you carry a camera," Merilee Rowling said.

"What?" I responded, annoyed by her interruption. "It's sort of a hobby."

"I was wondering if I could use it to get a picture of Chief Eagle Dog," she said.

"Chief Leopard Frog," I corrected her.

"That's the guy," she agreed. "Do you mind? I haven't been issued a camera yet, and I know it would help the story if I could get a picture of him in his, like, native habitat, so to speak. Does he live in a tepee?"

"No," I replied. "He most definitely does not live in a tepee."

"Well, maybe we could get him to stand in front of a tepee. How would he feel about that?" she asked.

"I'm pretty sure he wouldn't like it," I replied, "but I don't speak for Chief Leopard Frog. Maybe if you drove to Wal-Mart and bought him a tepee he'd stand in front of it. I don't know. I can't imagine why he would, but he's his own person."

"Is he, now?" Merilee Rowling pressed. "That's not the way your mother describes it."

She was standing so close that I could smell her breath. It smelled like peppermint and cinnamon and young woman.

"My mother and Chief Leopard Frog are not close," I declared. "I wouldn't expect her to know what he likes and doesn't like."

"But you do," Merilee Rowling continued. "You can interpret things for him, right? Like Don Diego can interpret things for Zorro. Or Clark Kent knows the whereabouts of Superman. Or Peter Parker can take us straight to Spider-Man. Or Bruce Wayne has deep insights into Batman. C'mon, Spencer, give me a break. I've got an Indian poet story to write and no Indian poet in sight."

"Let's take a walk," I said, grabbing my camera bag.

"By all means," Merilee Rowling agreed.

We set out across the pasture toward the Lambert place. There once were a dozen Lamberts living there, but today, of course, there are none.

The Lamberts kept ponies, rabbits, chickens, and ducks. For extra money they cut timber—hardwoods—which at one time they had a lot of, but the inevitable day came when they had none at all. All of it had been turned into corrugated boxes and sold to the Chinese so the Chinese could pack the stuff they sell to America.

Then, like everybody else in Paisley, Kansas, the Lamberts pulled up stakes, put their place up for sale, which nobody in their right mind would buy, and moved to Kansas City, where I heard from my mother that Mr. Lambert was working as an assistant manager in an envelope factory run by a former mayor.

"I could take your picture," I said.

"Sure," Merilee Rowling replied. "Maybe the magazine would publish it with my byline."

"Stand over there by that rusted tractor. That's kind of interesting," I said.

"Okay," Merilee Rowling agreed.

I sighted through the lens. Instead of going macro, up close, like I'd do for a grasshopper, or a stinkbug, I switched to telephoto, what's called a long lens, in order to blur out the background and focus exclusively on the face of the subject.

In many ways, this improved an already attractive young woman's appearance. It smoothed out imperfections in her skin while calling attention to her made-up eyes, her pert nose, and her lightly painted smile, all of which were quite appealing.

From where I stood, Merilee Rowling looked like the cover of a glossy European magazine, such as the Italian version of *Vogue* or possibly the French edition of *Vanity Fair.*

Pretty but exotically standoffish.

I squeezed the trigger again and again, each time capturing a slightly different aspect of her visual personality. When the short roll of film was exhausted, I exchanged it for a fresh one, slipping the exposed cylinder into the pocket of my jeans.

"Well?" she said. "How'd I do?"

"You looked great," I told her. "I can't wait to get them processed."

"Okay, now let me take your picture," she insisted.

"Do you know anything about cameras?" I asked warily.

"Oh, Spencer," she sighed. "Why are you so distrustful of everyone? Is it because you live in the wilderness all by yourself? Give me the stupid camera!"

Memo to self: When a woman impatiently insists, beware!

A Crack in the World

MERILEE ROWLING had put her foot down and I had accepted the gesture like an ant in a long, curving trail to honey.

I handed her my father's camera loaded with a fresh roll of film. The sun was only halfway up the sky so the light was still good.

"Let's go to that rundown barn," she directed.

She was referring to the lean-to that the Lamberts had built as a shelter for their ponies. Made from cedar, it was never painted, so it looked older than it actually was. There were three stalls and a tack room inside, and the lock on the tack room had left with the Lamberts. It was an appealing set for someone interested in making interesting photographs.

"Stand over there," she directed, in front of an open stall. "Now put your arm on the stall door and gaze out to your right."

"This feels weird," I said.

"This is art," Merilee Rowling insisted. "It's supposed to feel weird.

"Okay, ready?" she said. "One, two, three—oh, crap!"

Merilee Rowling had dropped the camera onto a concrete base poured for a hitching post that had never been installed. On impact, the film popped out of the back, exposed to the sunlight, and the lens cracked like a dried duck egg.

"Damn!" she said. "Why did you move?"

"I didn't move," I replied. "I'm still right here with my arm on the stall door."

"Well, somebody moved," she insisted. "Maybe it was your mysterious Indian."

"Is the camera okay?" I asked.

"Well," Merilee Rowling answered, "it might need a little adjustment."

I examined the case for damage.

I sighted through the viewfinder. On a single-lens reflex camera such as this one, the viewfinder reveals exactly what the lens sees, and what the lens now saw was a mixed-up, multifaceted universe.

It was exactly like looking through a kaleidoscope.

Merilee's image was broken into a star-shaped pattern of bits and pieces and the weedy fields around her appeared as a tan, circular sky.

If I changed the adjustment, say from macro to telephoto, the quiltlike pattern changed also, but the problem with the picture did not go away.

My ghost camera—my father's ghost camera—had been what an adjuster from State Farm Insurance (Auto-Home-Life) might classify as "totaled."

"Who sent you?" I asked angrily.

"Sorry," Merilee Rowling said.

"Here," I replied petulantly, handing her the pony talisman that Chief Leopard Frog had recently given to me. "This is for you. It was handmade by Chief Leopard Frog. Now, if you'll ask me the questions you need to ask about him, I'll do my best to answer."

"Can he fly?" she giggled, pocketing the amulet. "Does he have X-ray vision?"

She went running into the pony barn, and for some reason performed a cartwheel.

"How long are you planning to stay?" I asked her.

"How long would you like me to stay?" she replied coquettishly.

"Are you really seventeen?" I asked.

"I can prove it. It's on my driver's license," she answered. "Are you really nineteen?"

"No," I answered. "But I'm old enough to know what you're up to."

"And what is that, Mr. Wise Guy?" she flirted.

"You're trying to get me to make you as famous as Chief Leopard Frog and you don't mind wrecking my life in the process, starting with my camera," I observed.

Merilee Rowling put her hands on her hips and stared at me.

"You *are* a smart boy," she observed. "Will you guard my room again tonight?"

Man, was I ever in over my head.

Help, Chief Leopard Frog! I cried inside. *Help!*

"I guess so," I agreed, ever the weakling.

Walking home I spied a silver Yukon speeding down the dusty gravel road in the distance. In most parts of the world this would mean nothing. But if you were in Antarctica, let's say, it would be an event worth noting in your daily log. As I have previously suggested, Paisley has a lot in common with Antarctica, except instead of penguins we have locusts. But like other remote spots on the globe, we have very few people, and thus very few cars.

"Look at that hot rod go," Merilee Rowling observed. "How could anybody around here be in a hurry? I mean, what's the rush?"

"I think it all depends on whether they're coming or going," I suggested.

But of course I knew.

I recognized the car.

It was the Baldersons. And, no doubt, Maureen Balderson was inside.

I had a lot of explaining to do.

The Vertical Insect

MERILEE ROWLING AND I walked into my mother's kitchen.

"What happened to your camera?" she asked.

"Gravity," I replied gravely.

"Let me take a look," Dwight Earl offered, wiping his hands on an apron with a big smiley sun face that said BLESS THIS GLORIOUS GOD-GIVEN MORNING!

"Broken lens," he observed. "Anything else?"

"Not that I know of," I replied.

"With a camera like this," he explained, "lenses are interchangeable. They're not cheap, but lots of places sell used lenses. You might be able to replace it."

"And you were all ready to be mad at me," Merilee Rowling cooed. "See how easily problems can be solved if you keep a cool head about you?"

"I don't think that's the lesson to be learned here, Merilee," I replied. "I think the lesson may have something to do with carelessness with other people's property."

"Mmm," she responded, abruptly changing the subject. "Those waffles smell simply delightful!"

"Help yourself," Dwight Earl offered. "I'm making enough for the people next door, too."

"They're coming here?" I said, startled.

I did not want Maureen Balderson to meet Merilee Rowling. Their getting together seemed like putting two of Chief Leopard Frog's bad luck omens together in a bag and then hoping for the best.

"Your mother thought it would be a nice gesture," Dwight Earl explained. "They're in town for just a little while."

"I'd better pack up this roll of film for processing," I said. "I'll see you guys later."

Oh, man, I thought. *What if Merilee Rowling tells Maureen that we sleep in the same room? Or what if Maureen lets on that there's more to this deal than just neighbors? Dang, dang, and double dang! Why must things be so complicated?*

Coward that I am when it comes to confronting women whose ages are out of range of my own, I stayed in my room to work on my camera.

Carefully, I took it apart and cleaned it, using both special silicone-impregnated tissues and canned compressed air.

Tiny bits of film from countless trips through the sprockets flew out, along with an alarming amount of dust and grit. The lens itself, of course, was a total loss, although it still fit securely onto the lens mount. I made a note of the brand, model number, and type of lens in case I could find a store that could replace it.

But whatever paranormal capabilities my father's camera might have had surely were lost when it landed on the concrete.

Or, I suddenly thought with alarm, *if not then, then when I cleaned it so thoroughly.*

Now what I had was a camera that was as good as new—but with a shattered, useless lens.

To prove my point, I loaded it with a fresh roll of film and went downstairs, where a party of sorts was in progress.

All four of the Baldersons had arrived. I wondered if Tim had killed any wildlife on his way over—stomped on a lizard, thrown a rock at a hummingbird, set fire to a spider.

His father was chatting with the FedEx man about what a rush he must always be in, while his mother was telling my mother about how many shoe stores, tanning salons, dry cleaners, and drive-through banks there were in Kansas City.

"There's even a store that's as big as a high school gymnasium that sells nothing but containers!" Mrs. Balderson gushed. "Can you imagine?"

"I don't know how you'd ever decide," my mother replied.

"I can't figure out where to put all the stuff she brings home," her husband interrupted, laughing warmly. "We may have to get a bigger house."

"My company delivers a lot of packages from those stores," Dwight Earl chimed in, as if anybody cared.

Speaking of nobody caring, it did not escape my notice that no one said, "Oh, there he is," upon my arrival.

They all just kept on doing what they were doing.

In the case of Merilee Rowling and Maureen Balderson, it was just as I had feared. They were gossiping a mile a minute, apparently about boys, while Tim was spraying Windex on a trail of ants near the flip-top kitchen garbage can.

Just for fun, I popped up the built-in flash, focused as best I could on the scene in front of me, attempting to place Maureen and Merilee in the center so the others would fan out around them like a rose window in an ancient cathedral, and snapped the shutter.

Click-thunk!

For a brief millisecond in time, caught by the flash, everyone stopped talking and looked in my direction. Then, seeing that it was (only) me with my camera, they immediately picked up where they'd left off, like a skip in a record, or a hiccup in an otherwise boring speech.

Interesting, I thought. *At last I have succeeded in becoming the fly on the wall.*

Movers and Shakers of Kansas History

THE TRUE ARTIST takes advantage of every opportunity.

Having been relegated to little more than wallpaper by the guests in my own home, I hastened to make photographs, all abstract yet geometrically perfect. A face repeated a dozen times in fragments within my field of vision.

It was as if I really were a fly, or a grasshopper, or a honeybee—a multilensed, superior-sighted insect such as I'd photographed so carefully so long ago in the pumpkin patch.

Switching to macro mode, I tried again to capture what the shattered lens could see. Merilee Rowling laughing, her lips repeated dozens of times in a circle. Maureen Balderson with her tongue sticking out at me, again, multiplied by every break in the lens into a precise circular pattern of mathematical equality. Dwight Earl's eyebrows. My mother's handsome profile. The Baldersons' sandal-shod feet. Tim Balderson crawling on the floor to smash a cockroach with his fist.

It occurred to me that if these kaleidoscopic pictures actually turned out, I might have something resembling art.

"All art depends on happy accidents," I recall Chief Leopard Frog telling me.

Perhaps he should apply that same philosophy to his book of poetry, I thought. Burl Hives, *indeed!*

It also occurred to me that during the past twenty-four hours the population of Paisley, Kansas, had increased threefold, and that's not even counting Chief Leopard Frog, who will always remain a special case.

Spiritual leader of the uncounted.

Statistically speaking, I calculated, at this moment, Paisley is the fastest-growing town in Kansas.

If there were a newspaper in town, I would notify them of the event.

As it was, I merely helped myself to a waffle.

Interesting, I thought, as the sweet maple-flavored corn syrup awakened my taste buds, *how a place that only a moment ago lay in complete ruins, like some latter-day Pompeii buried by bad luck and human neglect, could suddenly become so warm and bustling with laughter and chatter.*

"Hello, stranger," Maureen Balderson said, at last breaking free from the ironclad verbal grip of Merilee Rowling. "Miss me?"

"I miss everything," I replied. "But what can I do about it?"

"You could move away like everybody else," she suggested.

"No. We're stuck," I explained. "Nobody would ever buy our house and my mother needs her job. Even though it's a phony-baloney government job, it pays regular money."

"Did you know that in the olden days, when towns in Kansas were bypassed by the railroad by twenty miles or so, that the townspeople would pick up and move the entire town?" Maureen Balderson asked rhetorically.

"The people?" I said. "Well, sure, the people would move."

"The buildings, too," she added. "Everything. Stone buildings, brick buildings, wood buildings, you name it. They put them on log rollers or cut them apart and hauled them on wagons.

"In the olden days," she continued, her voice becoming louder, "people just went to where they needed to so they could make things work, like the Native Americans who kept moving their tepees while following the buffalo."

"I'm not sure I understand your point," I said.

"You may be the last kid in Paisley, Kansas, Spencer Honesty," she said, placing her hand on my shoulder, "but you don't have to always be the last kid in town."

All of a sudden tears welled up in my eyes again, and try as I might I could not stop crying.

What a blubbering machine I had become!

Just call me Spencer Boo-hoo-hoo.

Maureen Balderson took me by the hand and led me outside to the porch, away from the others, then, saying nothing, put her arms around me and permitted me to cry against her shoulder for a full five minutes.

When at last I had exhausted my emotion, I saw that her shirt was stained with my tears.

She didn't seem to mind.

In the far distance down the gravel road, Chief Leopard Frog stood watching us. When he saw that I had spotted him, he raised his right hand and waved, sort of like the pope might wave to a crowd from His Holiness's private balcony. I took it to be Chief Leopard Frog's gesture of blessing.

"So when do you go back to Kansas City?" I asked.

"We're leaving this afternoon," Maureen explained. "Dad just wanted to be sure the house was okay, and Tim hadn't gotten to kill anything but houseflies and mosquitoes lately. It's only a few hours' drive. You ought to come see us sometime."

"I'd like to," I said, "but I can't drive myself and the Greyhound doesn't stop in Paisley anymore."

"You're a smart boy," Maureen Balderson said. "You'll think of something."

This time she kissed me on the mouth, deeply, tenderly, as if I were the only boy in the world.

Then she posed for me as I repeatedly took her picture with the kaleidoscope camera.

Click-thunk! Click-thunk! Click-thunk!

The Business World

MERILEE ROWLING stayed over one more night. I slept in my nest on the floor beside her bed. She asked me as many questions about Maureen Balderson as she did about Chief Leopard Frog. I spun yarns about both.

I told her Maureen Balderson was Chief Leopard Frog's illegitimate daughter, that she was actually a princess in the Sac and Fox tribe, and that she had helped her father get his first book of poetry published by the leading publishing company in the Cayman Islands by trading a priceless necklace made of wolves' teeth.

I found the snapshot that I had made of Chief Leopard Frog and gave it to Merilee Rowling to publish in her magazine. I explained to her that Chief Leopard Frog lived off the land and preferred to stay out of sight, hiding in abandoned houses, of which there were many, except when he had a bundle of poems to deliver. That's when he'd come to see my mother and me, because we knew how to use the U.S. mail and he, being a primitive, didn't.

I explained to Merilee Rowling that all of Paisley was once Indian territory but it was taken away from them by unscrupulous late-nineteenth-century railroad barons, who tricked the Native Americans into thinking that they would get free passes to ride in the plush sleeping cars forever.

I could hear Merilee Rowling scribbling very fast in her notebook. Eventually, I got sleepy and forgot the exact details of the blarney that I was spewing.

Finally both Merilee Rowling and I fell asleep. By then it must have been well past midnight.

The next day when I awoke I remembered having told Merilee Rowling that I had been married to Maureen Balderson in a Sac and Fox ceremony under a hedgeapple tree but that the marriage could not be made legal until I turned eighteen. This "fact" didn't exactly fly with Merilee Rowling.

At one point during the evening she had gotten up to go to the bathroom and stepped on my leg. On the way back, she stepped on my leg again and fell down on top of me. At that moment we were both on the floor, our bodies touching, face to face.

"You're a cute kid," Merilee Rowling said, "but I think you're not the one for me."

"Well, good night again," I said.

"Good night, Spencer," she replied. "What a strange life you live."

As she was getting up to climb back into bed, Chief Leopard Frog walked into the room, picked up my camera, and took our picture with the broken lens.

"Yi!" Merilee Rowling screamed. "This place is freaking haunted."

"I'll take care of it," I assured her.

"What's going on in there?" my mother hollered.

"Bad dreams," I called back. "Good night."

Merilee Rowling left just after a great country breakfast that consisted of naturally cured ham, biscuits and gravy, and homemade apple butter. I helped her pack up her stuff and stood like a hitching post in the driveway while she pulled onto the gravel road. She honked the horn twice and was gone. That's when it dawned on me that she was wearing my peach-colored Columbus Catfish baseball cap, the one that had been my father's.

Such treachery from a trusted houseguest! I thought. *Why, it's downright Shakespearean.*

Code of honor, indeed!

At least Paisley was back to being Paisley.

The weather had changed. Now the early mornings were cool, with a patchy fog, which for years I had thought was called Apache fog given my orientation to Indians and my limited homeschool education.

The pumpkins were ripe, the spiders fewer in number, and one morning there was frost on the three mailboxes.

I threw myself into business, shipping the last of the celebrity look-alike pumpkins to Milton Swartzman and another gross of bad luck talismans carved by Chief Leopard Frog. I also sent on the poetry book orders for him to handle according to the terms of our contract, keeping only a dozen copies of the book for myself.

The money was rolling in.

A fortnight later Dwight Earl the FedEx man showed up for lunch with a big package under his arm. It was from Sparkle Snapshot in St. Louis.

A letter was glued onto the outside of the box.

It was from the office of the president of Sparkle Snapshot.

Dear Valued Customer, it read.

As you know, here at Sparkle Snapshot we take great care in what we do. Indeed, we have processed some of the best of the best from the world's finest photographers: Annie Leibovitz's cross-eyed sister, Sally Anne; Diane Arbus's cataract-challenged mother, Louise; Gordon Parks's blind cousin, LaFrange O'Reilly; Walker Evans's next-door neighbor Big Turley Hawthorne, to cite but a few.

That's why, in 1974, we established the Sparkle Foundation and the Annual Sparkle Snapshot Award to call attention to our customers' achievements and to encourage the pursuit of photographic excellence.

Your photograph "Romeo and Juliet" has been selected as this year's winner. Congratulations! You may be pleased to learn that the judges' decision was unanimous.

What can I say?

You could have knocked me over with a lens tissue.

A Prizewinning Photographer

THE PRESIDENT of Sparkle Snapshot was not yet finished with his accolades:

Enclosed you will find a sixteen-by-twenty-inch mounted repro-duction of your winning picture, he wrote, *a check representing your prize money, and a document for you to sign and return granting Sparkle Snapshot Service permission to publicize your photograph through the professional art and photography community in the United States, its territories and possessions, and sovereign and emerg-ing nations abroad.*

With sincere admiration,

Lance L. Leiberman

President

Sparkle Snapshot Service

P.S. Your regular processing order follows by U.S. mail.

P.P.S. Again, congratulations. This is extraordinary work.

Inside, mounted on heavy art board, was a big color kaleido-scopic photograph of Merilee Rowling and me in what appeared to be a lovers' embrace as seen through the multifaceted eye of a hovering honeybee.

The color was intense; the design, repeated over and over in nearly identical fragments, like wallpaper, only intensified the feeling that the viewer had accidentally stumbled into an intensely private world.

If you looked closely, you could see the ghost image of Chief Leopard Frog repeated as well in the form of a portrait hanging on the wall in the background. I could also make out my peach-colored ball cap hung on the doorknob and Mr. Riley's dead dog Flag watching over us like a hundred tiny sentries.

I had to admit, it was a remarkable piece of art—and the greatest achievement of the ghost camera to date. The only problem with it was that I didn't take the picture.

Chief Leopard Frog did.

But the check for one hundred thousand dollars was payable to me. There were also a dozen half-price coupons for additional film processing, which I thought was a nice gesture, and there was a handsome walnut and brass wall plaque, too.

Well, I thought to myself, *you just never know when your luck is going to change.*

I just wish it had been Maureen Balderson in the photo instead of Merilee Rowling. Something told me there would be trouble later on.

"Mom," I asked my mother, as we dined on chicken-fried steak at the table with Dwight Earl, who, I noticed, kept his FedEx uniform cap on even when inside the house, "have you ever considered putting our house on log rollers and moving it about two hundred and fifty miles to Kansas City?"

"No, I can't say that I ever have," she replied, sopping a biscuit into the white gravy. "How about you, Dwight Earl? That thought ever cross your mind?"

"Not even once," he answered. "Not even back when I was a drinking man."

"Well, it's good that you saw the light," my mother concluded approvingly.

"I'll be in my room," I announced, taking my plate to the sink.

First, I wrote a formal thank-you note to Lance L. Leiberman, in appreciation of the outstanding honor and award as well as the many useful half-price certificates.

I assured him I would tell everybody in town about the fine quality of his film services.

That wouldn't take long.

Then I began a letter to the only worldly-wise adult I knew, Milton Swartzman, president and publisher of *Uncle Milton's Thousand Things You Thought You'd Never Find*. In it, I told him about how my camera had gotten broken and how it had resulted in my winning a snapshot prize. I didn't mention how much money was involved. No point in getting Uncle Milton all worked up.

I held on to the letter for a couple of days until the regular mail brought the packet from Sparkle Snapshot that had all the new kaleidoscopic work in it. It was truly a treasure trove of surprises. I enclosed one sample for Milton Swartzman to help him understand the new technique.

As for the packet of pictures, it held my attention for hours. There was an entire roll devoted to Merilee Rowling prancing around like a glamour model, prior to the damage to the lens. I had to admit that even though she was a swindler and a liar and a hat thief and a con artist and a tease, she was a good-looking young woman. Eventually, somebody would settle down to make a life with her just because of her looks.

Boy, would he ever be sorry!

To demonstrate that I'm a good sport, I picked out half a dozen of the best shots and sent them to her in care of *Poetry Week* magazine. Maybe my gesture would encourage her to write something nice about Paisley.

The second roll of film was like being inside the Dalí Museum for the first time in your life or discovering the mind and drawings of M. C. Escher or possibly seeing your first painting by Henri Matisse or Gustav Klimt.

It was an unexpected immersion into a mini-collection of truly original startling art, if I do say so myself.

Nothing in life could have adequately prepared me for what I now witnessed.

Fantasy Begets Fame

ALTHOUGH NO ONE HAS ASKED, I offer a few words of explanation about my prizewinning photograph.

I had begun by attempting to take pictures of the macro world, the world that's the size of a bug. I'd wound up photographing the human world as bugs see it, with the addition of a few phantoms thrown in for atmosphere.

My portrait of Maureen Balderson after she kissed me is the one that should have won the prize. Her image was glorious, equal slivers of herself woven together into a tapestry and glowing like the sun.

I could understand the judges' choosing the one with Merilee Rowling, the one they labeled "Romeo and Juliet" (how did they come up with that?), because it "told a story," however false, something that photo judges seem to like. But for sheer beauty, Maureen Balderson's image was the winner in my book, hands down.

Immediately, I used one of the half-price coupons to order enlargements of the portrait for Maureen and myself. Then, while I was at it, I ordered duplicates of the entire roll to share with Milton Swartzman.

As things were turning out, I could afford as many copies as I wanted.

By the time the overgrown pastures of Paisley turned honey brown and blue ice had formed at the edges of the ponds, I received a letter from Milton Swartzman sharing my appreciation for the work made possible by the broken ghost camera and suggesting that we publish a volume of photos for national release.

Such printing is very expensive, he advised me. *Doing color work takes many steps, superior paper, quality craftsmen, and an editorial understanding of the artist's intentions. It is also typically done in short runs, which are more expensive as well, at least on a cost-per-book basis.*

Thus, the best I can offer you is fifteen percent of the gross receipts, he explained. *I hope this is acceptable to you. I think you have something important to share, and I am trying very hard to be fair. Not so easy after all these years.*

Ever the businessman, Uncle Milton enclosed a contract, which I signed and returned to him with a note of thanks.

Meanwhile, the latest issue of *Poetry Week* magazine was published, which would have escaped me altogether had I not noticed it on the side table by the mortgage department desk while depositing my monthly Milton Swartzman check in the bank across the street from Wal-Mart.

"May I borrow this?" I asked.

"Take it," the mortgage banker insisted. "The last poem anybody around here gave a pig's patooie about was 'Casey at the Bat.'"

"Thanks," I said. "I'll get it back to you."

"Not necessary," he insisted. "Just don't take the copy of *Entertainment Weekly,* the 'Top Twenty-five Starlets Under Age Twenty-five' issue. I'm not done with it yet."

"How about *Photo World*?" I asked, detecting that the mortgage banker was in a generous mood. "Anybody need that one?"

"Not unless it has naked ladies in it," he advised. "Let me take a quick look."

Apparently it didn't, because he let me have it as well.

Back home, armed with a fresh supply of contemporary reading material, I made myself comfortable in my nest, which, thankfully, had been returned to the top of the bed. Curiously, it still smelled strongly of Merilee Rowling's flowery perfume, a scent I since have learned is called L'Air du Temps by Nina Ricci.

I don't speak French, but I sense the combination of air and time.

My mother, of course, was too busy watching *Oprah* to be bothered with laundry, and I for one didn't really care. As long as it didn't stink, I figured, I could live with it.

It didn't. I could.

Merilee Rowling's story of Chief Leopard Frog and his breakthrough book of poems, *Burl Hives*, was a grandiose fiction from start to finish.

Merilee claimed to have spent the night with Chief Leopard Frog in his tepee under a full moon in a wheat field in Paisley, Kansas.

She said she'd met his daughter and her white husband of the heavens, who had presented her with a magic horse-shaped amulet that could predict the future.

She claimed to have been inducted into the Sac and Fox tribe in a ceremony involving waffles cooked on a raging prairie fire set by lightning.

It was a shameless, self-indulgent fabrication, and she included as proof of her presence one of the photos I'd sent showing her posing near the rusted tractor.

Her article reproduced twelve of Chief Leopard Frog's poems in their entirety, a copyright infringement that was as outrageous as the rest of her story.

She properly described Paisley as a ghost town, but went on to say that one peculiar family still held on, clinging to illusions, in a falling-down house that was haunted by generations of Native Americans.

She described my mother as a baffled, harried, and forgotten employee of the Bureau of Indian Affairs, and me as a diminutive teenager whose hormones had overtaken his mind.

She expressed pity for our condition and predicted a bright future for Chief Leopard Frog. She included his picture in the story. The credit line for the photo read "Photo by Merilee Rowling."

It was, in fact, just what I expected, and sales of *Burl Hives* doubled overnight. The checks from the Cayman Islands began arriving daily.

You never know.

Sore Legal Eagles Soar

SUCH A LITTLE scam artist!

I sent Merilee Rowling a postcard. It said, *Dear Stranger: Read your story. Nice work. Please return my daddy's hat or I'm telling on you. Your pal, Spencer.*

Photo World was even more interesting.

My prizewinning photo was on the cover. Inside, a brief article consisting of quotes from Mr. Leiberman and an assistant professor at St. Louis University named Jay Schmo, Ph.D., declared that a new branch had burst forth on the evolutionary tree of the visual arts. An exhibition in New York was predicted but no details were provided.

How do people get away with such stuff?

How do the disseminators of facts continue to engage in such egregious half-truths and falsehoods?

Is the whole world made up of liars?

Uncle Milton sent me a twelve-thousand-dollar advance on the book of photos. He had titled it *Inside a Bug's Eye,* which I thought was fairly restrictive, but when *Newsweek* magazine picked a portion of the collection for a special issue and the bonus check arrived, I couldn't have cared less if he'd called it *Inside a Bug's Ass.*

The money kept pouring in.

Who's the girl you're rolling around with in Newsweek? Maureen Balderson questioned me on a postcard bearing an image of a hay bale wearing oversize sunglasses with the headline "LIFE IS A BEACH IN KANSAS." *It looks a lot like that strumpet Merilee Rowling that I met at your house. What's happened to you? Always, MO.*

Immediately, I sent off a reply, also on a postcard, this one a split image showing wild turkeys happily gobbling in a field on the left half while on the right half they were being carried like gray flour sacks flung over the shoulders of two men with shotguns. It bore the headline "LIFE IS A SPORT IN KANSAS!"

It's not what it seems, I swear, I wrote to Maureen Balderson. *I am a victim of unscrupulous business opportunists. She means nothing to me. Less than nothing. Just a prop for a picture. Love, Spencer.*

Not that I'd been all that scrupulous.

But the fact is, you don't get to be a big success without cutting a few people off at the knees when the situation calls for it, and having a smart lawyer for a brother, or having a friend who has a smart lawyer for a brother.

Milton Swartzman's brother was a big shot lawyer in Palm Beach, Florida. His name was Howard. His office was on the top floor of a bank building that overlooked the surging Atlantic Ocean.

From his office, Howard Swartzman looked down not only on everybody else in Palm Beach but also on many rich Europeans arriving on private yachts and cruise ships.

With Howard's help, I was able to stop Merilee Rowling from getting the money for the movie rights to Chief Leopard Frog's story, which Universal Studios had offered seventeen million dollars for, based on her fascinating and widely read article in the once obscure *Poetry Week.*

The case was unique in the annals of copyright law and eventually became known as the "Frog Decision."

The judgment hinged on this point: A heavily fictionalized story about an imaginary person, when presented as legitimate journalistic fact, is wholly dependent upon the imaginary person's actual existence. Inasmuch as the imaginary person in *Honesty versus Rowling*, namely, Chief Leopard Frog, was imagined entirely by Honesty and not at all by Rowling, the imaginary character is the exclusive property of Honesty.

The court compared the case to Walt Disney's imaginary creation of Mickey Mouse. Many artists drew the character in various settings and with various appearances, but to this day Mickey Mouse remains the exclusive property of Walt Disney, his heirs, and his assigns.

Although Rowling owns the copyright to her actual written words, in their unique sequence and configuration, the court explained, she is prohibited from exploiting the imaginative creation of Honesty known as C. L. Frog.

In other words: *Girl, get your own imaginary friend!*

You can't steal another person's delusions and expect to get away with it—not in this litigious day and age.

Additionally, Howard Swartzman was able to extract a very generous compensation from the well-endowed *Poetry Week* magazine for its unauthorized publication of Chief Leopard Frog's poems.

When Merilee Rowling tried to countersue for my failure to obtain a model release for the use of her image in my prizewinning photo, Howard-the-lawyer threatened to charge her with the theft of my peach-colored Columbus Catfish ball cap, a serious federal crime since the hat had traveled across state lines in violation of the Baseball Fann Act.

Her case against me immediately collapsed.

Clearly, genius runs in Uncle Milton's family.

Howard then sued *Photo World* for failing to pay me for use of the cover photo, went after FedEx for routinely delaying my shipments, and, quite by accident, filed suit against his own brother for a number of contract violations involving the talismans, the pumpkins, and the books, but when that inadvertent action came to light we all quietly settled over an excellent home-cooked meal prepared by my mother. As I recall, it included chicken livers.

Afterward, as a gesture of kindness, Milton gave Howard the Sammy Davis, Jr., pumpkin for his office in Palm Beach, where, I understand, it is much admired by his wealthy clientele.

Peace prevaileth, so to speaketh.

All's Well That Has a New Beginning

MY PICTURE BOOK, now in its seventeenth printing, was going gangbusters. It had become especially popular in Holland, Germany, Denmark, Sweden, and France.

Autographed reproductions of my photos, prepared at Sparkle Snapshot in St. Louis, Missouri, and mounted on fine art board by an outfit in Sri Lanka (to reduce labor costs, Mr. Leiberman explained), were selling for more than five thousand dollars apiece plus shipping and handling.

Mr. Leiberman took care of everything for a mere twenty-five percent.

The bank across the highway from the Wal-Mart sent me a personalized rubber stamp to endorse my checks so my hand wouldn't get tired when making all my deposits. They also let me select twenty magazine subscriptions free from a list provided by the bank vice president's daughter, who was selling subscriptions to benefit her high school band.

I'll probably never get around to reading *Cigar Aficionado*, but as long as it didn't cost me anything, I figured I'd add it to the pile. I also checked off *O*, Oprah's magazine, and *TV Guide*, both for my mother, plus the new *Reader's Digest*, because it fit so neatly on the back of the toilet.

What I was really looking forward to receiving, however, was *Kansas Real Estate Investor Monthly*, because I had big plans percolating.

I was, by now, the richest kid in town. A dubious achievement given the population of Paisley, but worth mentioning.

Just as paper covers rock, and rock breaks scissors, and scissors cut paper, so does business activity mask loneliness. In fact, there is a point at which business activity masks everything, from ethics to love.

I had forgotten to write back to Maureen Balderson.

It had been weeks since the last exchange of postcards.

No, it was worse than that. I looked it up. It had been months. I'd been too busy getting rich to remember that the former girl next door was about to celebrate her sixteenth birthday.

Being rich does not guarantee to make you happy, but if you've figured out a way to make someone else happy, being rich definitely helps you express your feelings.

As it turned out, the Baldersons' house in Kansas City was part of a suburban real estate development adjacent to what only recently had been a farm occupied exclusively by wild rabbits and coyotes.

Now, of course, it was a prime site for a housing development for sale to any fool who would pay the asking price of sixty thousand dollars an acre, an outrageous sum for land by Paisley standards.

I bought all forty acres of it.

I also bought the Baldersons' house in Paisley. Then I arranged with Happy Turtle House Movers of Pittsburg, Kansas (down here, there is no *h* in Pittsburg), to have it moved to my land in Kansas City, where it was carefully situated on a pretty, partially wooded half-acre lot next door to the Baldersons' new house.

A little brass plaque on the front door read HAPPY BIRTHDAY SWEET SIXTEEN.

Mrs. Balderson was thrilled. Not only did she now have enough room to put away all the stuff she'd been buying at the stores in Kansas City, but she knew exactly where it all would fit.

Maureen Balderson was speechless, but her tears of joy said it all.

"Oh, Spencer," she finally murmured.

Her father put his arm around me and tormented me briefly with a half bear hug while Tim went tearing down the street after a rabbit that had been flushed from the bushes by all the activity.

As dramatic as this gesture was, however, it was only the beginning.

Within two months the entire town of Paisley, Kansas, had been rolled two hundred and fifty miles down the highway and planted like winter wheat in the fertile land of Kansas City's newest upscale subdivision, Paisley Paradise.

In the center of the development, in a beautifully proportioned red-brick Georgian building reminiscent of the College of William and Mary in Williamsburg, Virginia, stood the Louise Franks Memorial Free Library of Paisley, Kansas.

Surrounding it were Mr. Heath's general merchandise store, the Honesty Gallery of Contemporary Art, Baskin-Robbins, Pizza Hut, PetSmart, OfficeMax, Subway, and Bed Bath & Beyond.

(Give me a break! Every real estate developer has to make a *few* compromises!)

The Best That I Could Do

I MOVED THE WHOLE TOWN of Paisley, Kansas, to Maureen Balderson's new subdivision in Kansas City, but to my credit, I hope you realize, I did not move the plastics factory.

Neither, for that matter, did I bother to erect a statue to the town's founder and first mayor, the vagabond bandit Colonel Daschell Potts.

Instead, I commissioned a bigger-than-life bronze reproduction of an Indian chief leaning against a tree and whittling a talisman. My only regret is that through some hugely embarrassing mix-up, it got installed on a marble pedestal in front of the cigar store.

The hardest part in all of this was saying goodbye to the subject of the statue.

Chief Leopard Frog had not stood by me through thick and thin, but he'd certainly been with me through thin, which was when I'd needed him the most.

Without his native strength, his optimism, his wisdom, his creative gifts, his presence, and his confidence in me, I surely would have withered away like the once doomed town of Paisley.

We all owe so much to the native peoples who have gone before us.

"Won't you come with me?" I asked him as we stood side by side in a blustery wind on the vacant ground of Old Paisley.

"You know I can't," he replied. "You're merely being considerate of my feelings."

"Is that bad?" I asked. "Being considerate, I mean."

But already he was gone.

My mother somehow managed to keep her job delivering mail to the residents of Paisley now reestablished in its new location.

Who can fathom the collective bureaucratic mind of the United States government? Do they even have a clue? If so, does anybody care?

Today Paisley is filled with young couples and little kids and packs of odd-size, strange-behaving pedigreed dogs, teenagers with brand-new used cars, and a few slow strolling people in their twilight years who wear big smiles and wave to everyone whether they know them or not, some using canes and aluminum walkers.

Every year when the weather turns cold, I send a special pumpkin to Milton Swartzman. The last one looked just like President Franklin D. Roosevelt, glasses and all, I swear.

Oh, and guess who, at the tender age of nineteen, wound up becoming the fourth wife of Milton's brother Howard, the rich genius Palm Beach lawyer?

If you were about to say Merilee Rowling, you'd be absolutely right. But I wouldn't worry about him. He can afford her. The question is, how long can he stand her?

To my way of thinking, what Howard should have done is

gotten himself a dog, like I did: a little chestnut-colored miniature dachshund with short legs and a bobbed tail, full of frolic and kisses.

I named him Chief. We go everywhere together.

About the Author

Richard W. Jennings
www.richardwjennings.com

He is the "master of middle-American whimsy" according to *Kirkus Reviews*. The *Horn Book* explains, "He writes about children who are witty, intelligent, articulate, and likeable," and adds, "His novels are laced with droll tongue-in-cheek observations, philosophical musings, and slight hints of absurdity." The author says his work "celebrates the custodians of optimism—kids—and is dedicated to every kid who ever felt different."

Jennings's debut novel, *Orwell's Luck,* was launched to widespread critical acclaim in 2000, published in France as *La chance de ma vie* in 2001, and released through Houghton Mifflin and Scholastic Books as a trade paperback in 2006.

This success was followed at roughly annual intervals by *The Great Whale of Kansas* (2001), *My Life of Crime* (2002), *Mystery in Mt. Mole* (2003), *Scribble* (2004), *Stink City* (2006), *Ferret Island* (2007), and *The Pirates of Turtle Rock* (2008), praised by the professional media, and found in schools and libraries throughout the United States.

Several of Jennings's books have been excerpted or serialized in the *Kansas City Star,* including *Orwell's Luck, Scribble, Stink City, Ferret Island, The Pirates of Turtle Rock,* and his latest work, *Ghost Town.*

He shares his Overland Park, Kansas, home with three dachshunds—a bad one, a fat one, and a baby—where he writes full-time.